CRESS WATERCRESS

GREGORY MAGUIRE

CRESS WATERCRESS

ILLUSTRATED BY

DAVID LITCHFIELD

CANDLEWICK PRESS

Text copyright © 2022 by Kiamo Ko LLC
Illustrations copyright © 2022 by David Litchfield

First edition 2022

Library of Congress Catalog Card Number pending
ISBN 978-1-5362-1100-9

21 22 23 24 25 26 LGO 10 9 8 7 6 5 4 3 2 1

Printed in Vicenza, Italy

This book was typeset in Bell.
The illustrations were created digitally.

Candlewick Press
99 Dover Street
Somerville, Massachusetts 02144

www.candlewick.com

For Lucy Lark Prabhaker and
Maisy James Prabhaker
GM

For Katie, Benny, George, and Maggie
DL

CONTENTS

1

THE BARE WINDOWS OF HOME

Mama yanked down her homemade drapes and stuffed them into the carryall. The windows stared squarely out into the newness of how things were now. Mama said, "I think it is time." She pulled her apron strings tighter. She didn't look at her children. "Is everyone ready?"

Cress shrugged. Her mouth was dry, her words locked silent.

"You'll need to carry him, Cress," said Mama. "I have my arms full. Can you manage?"

Kip was disagreeable, all sour milk on salty soap. "NO GO."

"Don't fuss," said Mama. "This is hard enough. Be a good little bunny for Mama."

Kip threw himself in the middle of the empty warren. Gone now, the rag carpet that had made the floor soft. When Kip kicked, he hurt his feet. He cried harder.

Mama put down the map, the parcels tied in string, the carryall, the valise full of carrots. She picked up her little Kip. Since the rocking chair was gone, too, she rocked on her heels.

"Why won't you settle down, cuddles?" asked Mama. "I don't know what to do with you."

"He wants his stuffed carrot," said Cress.

"Want ROTTY," said Kip.

"I must have packed it and sent it ahead," said Mama.

"No," said Cress. "It's stuck in the hood of his onesie. Look, Kip! Here's your carrot."

"ROTTY," said Kip. There were more tears, and from more than one pair of eyes.

"And now we're ready," said Mama. Kip went into the snuggly. Cress grabbed Mama's paw and held on tight.

They left their home for the last time. No one bothered to lock the door or to look back at nobody waving goodbye.

2

DINNER BY MOONLIGHT

The setting sun was a lumpy clementine in a net bag of string clouds. The air, so cool and damp. A few birds moaned in falling tones. "Where are we going?" asked Cress.

"You'll see when we get there," said Mama crisply. Cress knew that was the end of talking for now.

Kip, sucking on the tip of his stuffed carrot, fell silent. But Cress thought she heard him murmur, "Papa?"

She couldn't bring herself to say, "No Papa," so she said, "Look, Kip. There's a little broken circle in the sky. Mama, is that the moon?"

"You've seen the moon before," said Mama. "You know the moon."

"I don't remember," said Cress. "You never let me go
out at night."

They didn't talk any more. The grass looked like dinner
and then it tasted like dinner. Dinner by moonlight, thought
Cress. Papa would love this.

Papa would have loved this.

3

WHERE WE'RE GOING

Mama had lost her map.

On the other side of the water, the ducks slept. They were too far away to wake up for directions.

Nearby, thorny branches tangled, a dark sword fight profiled against cliffs of silvery moon-cloud.

The family froze when Monsieur Reynard came by with a mouthful of hen, but his jaws were busy. He couldn't bother with Mama and her children tonight.

"We made it," said Cress as they hurried by, trying not to stare.

"Just luck," said Mama. "The fox had already chosen his meal."

"Do you think we should have helped that poor hen?" asked Cress.

"She was too dead, I'm afraid," replied Mama.

"Oh." Cress thought about it. "Did a fox get Papa?"

"Hush your lips!" Mama glanced at the baby. But Kip was asleep, dreaming of dipping carrots in honey.

Mama put her paw on Cress's shoulder. "We may never know what happened to Papa," she said. "But here we are, and the forest is home to more than one fox. So we must take care. If only I hadn't lost the map."

"Do you know where we're going?" asked Cress.

"Of course I know where we're going." Mama paused to stroke her whiskers and look around. "I just don't know the way."

4

AGATHA CABBAGE

I wish I knew what I did with the map," said Mama for the third time that night.

Cress said, "You left it on the floor when you were cuddling Kip."

"Why didn't you pick it up if you saw it lying there?" asked Mama.

"I wasn't in charge of the map," said Cress. "I can't be in charge of everything. I have the towels and the teaspoons. Not to mention Kip on my back." Cress didn't add that she had been too close to tears to speak.

"You should have pointed out that I dropped it." Mama tutted. Cress readied for a sound scolding. However, just then, a figure crossed their path in the moonlight, striping the horizon with black and white.

"Oh, my pearls and pistols. What do we have here? Humble country folk out for an evening stroll?" asked a lady skunk, peering through a lorgnette. "And far from home, by the look of your shabby luggage."

"Good evening, madame," said Mama.

"The little ones are out late," said the skunk. "I disapprove."

"Oh, do you?" asked Mama blandly. "Well, it can't be helped tonight."

"Not how I'd raise children, if I had any," replied the skunk. "But don't let me keep you. I'm off to the opera. Notice my lorgnette. Notice my chinchilla."

Wrapped around the skunk's neck, the chinchilla shyly lifted her head and murmured, "Howdy-do."

"Lady Agatha Cabbage is my name," said the skunk. She squinted through her eyepiece at Cress. "My, what a charming little girl you are. Little frou-frou, little bunny-kins, would you like to become my lady's maid? My last maid ran off. Useless. It's so hard to keep good help. Do come, child. I need help."

Cress was pretty brave but no way, no way. She pouted.

"Oh, she couldn't possibly," said her mother.

Lady Cabbage frowned and said, "I would give her sound training in manners, something you haven't managed to do yet."

Cress pressed her face into her mother's apron strings and held her breath.

"She's getting an education already," said Cress's mother. "She is homeschooled. Very well, I might add."

Lady Cabbage sniffed. "What could you possibly teach her at home school?"

"What home is," said her mother. She glanced about. "And where."

The skunk pushed the point. "But where is your home?"

"We were looking for a certain Mr. Owl who is said to have rooms to let," admitted Mama. "But we've lost our way."

"Mr. Owl? I know where that old crankcase lives," said the skunk. "I can show you. There are some nasty spiderwebs on the path. I suppose the opera can wait."

"You're too kind," said Cress's mother to Lady Cabbage.

The chinchilla twisted her head and whispered to Cress, "She's not that kind. She doesn't even like opera. She just likes to dress up and parade about."

"By the way," said Cress's mother, "a word to the wise. We just saw a fox go by with a mouthful of hen."

"I am scared of no fox," replied the skunk. "I have a powerful cologne that drives predators wild. You'll be safe with me. Come along."

"Just don't get on her stinky side," whispered the chinchilla.

5

THE GROWN-UP SORT
OF SECRETS

If Cress had ever been outside at night before, she had been too young to remember it.

Soft rain often misted her mornings. As if her mother had stayed up all night weaving the weather they wanted for a safe breakfast. Calm dawns turned into lazy afternoons, then blue and amber evenings.

But this vast night felt haunted with the grown-up sort of secrets. Pierced with silent watchings by hidden eyes. Or so Cress imagined.

Also sort of beautiful. Look, a scum-green pond with white glints bobbing on the wind-ruffled surface. "Mama?" asked Cress, pointing.

"That," said Mama, "is the reflection of the moon."

"Only one moon, but a thousand reflections!" said Cress.
"Like so many seeds spilled from one silver spoon!"

"My, but your girl is fanciful," remarked Lady Cabbage.
And then, "That could come in handy if she can tell stories."

"Keep close, Cress," said her mother.

"Not to get personal," asked the skunk, "but why are
you taking rooms in Mr. Owl's establishment? It's a bit of a
dump. A comedown."

"I don't like to talk about it." Cress's mother raised her

eyebrows meaningfully as if to signal: Not in front of the children.

"Do tell," urged the skunk. "As I live alone, I relish a chin-wag now and then."

Mama peered at the snuggly on Cress's back. Kip was asleep. He would hear nothing. His baby snores smelled like warm damp cotton.

"Go ahead, Mama," said Cress. "I can stand to hear it."

Mama said softly, "We were living in a proper warren on the riverbank. We ate at dawn and dusk, like most rabbits. Every now and then, my husband went out at night to find ginger root and honey for a tea I make."

"Divine," said Lady Cabbage insincerely.

"The tea is good for the baby, who often has trouble breathing. He'll outgrow his ailment. Probably." Mama sighed. "But one night last week, Papa went out and didn't come back."

"Husbands will do that," said Lady Cabbage. "Not that I know personally. I was never married."

"Not this husband," said Mama stoutly. "No, when Mr. Watercress failed to return at dawn, I felt in my bones that the worst had happened. A step too far in a dangerous direction. Trouble. Because nothing would keep my husband away but an untimely death."

The chinchilla wiped her damp eyes on the skunk's neck, but Lady Cabbage was too absorbed in the drama to notice.

Cress's mother spoke with determination: "I can't leave my children home alone at night. But I need to collect the honey and ginger root. So we're moving to a place where others live close by. Who may be helpful in a pinch. I heard from a sparrow that a basement flat at Mr. Owl's recently became available. I've taken it sight unseen. That's where we're going."

"Not to dampen your jollity," said Lady Cabbage, "but Mr. Owl isn't likely to be much help. He's not the baby-sitting type. Never budges an inch to help anyone."

"We don't have the privilege of choice," said Mama.

"Here is where we must stop listening to sad stories," said Lady Cabbage. "A certain tightly wound old snake lives under these rocks, or nearby. His nickname is the Final Drainpipe. He won't take kindly to being awakened by all this jabber."

"What's a drainpipe?" asked Cress.

"Hush, now," said Mama.

"Where you're going isn't the best neighborhood, I fear," said Lady Cabbage. "Down-market."

"You hush, too," said Mama to the skunk. This

surprised Cress, but the skunk fell silent. Which was something of a relief.

Cress looked and looked for the whiskery snub-nose of her father poking out from a shadowy clump of bracken. She kept not being able to see him. She could imagine him being there any minute, and the next minute, and the next. But he wasn't.

The slender moon became fretted by the branches of a dead tree. It looked like a sideways smile of broken teeth, which made Cress feel strange. Then the smile joined up again when they passed the tree. This also made Cress feel strange.

Everything made her feel strange.

Except the chinchilla, who was holding her nose because the skunk had just made a little odor of disapproval. That made Cress laugh.

6

LIGHT A CANDLE
IN THE DARKNESS

The little moon had climbed higher. The floor of the pine forest was crosshatched with brown needles. Walking on them raised up a smell like the balsam sachets Mama often made up for gifts.

"Just up this knoll and, voilà," said Lady Cabbage. "I won't say misery. I won't. Lips sealed. See for yourself."

They stood at the base of a towering old oak tree. Most of its smaller branches had fallen off. Perhaps it had been struck by lightning. Maybe more than once, until it had become a standing wreck of grey dead wood. Nothing green or lively about this place.

"Well, well," said Mama with an attempt at cheer. "I wonder if the landlord is home."

"Where would you expect me to be at this hour?" said a hoarse voice from above. The scratching of talons upon scarred bark.

They all looked up.

"Good evening, Mr. Owl," called the skunk. "It is I, Lady Cabbage, come to call."

"I know who it is," said the owl. "I could hear you coming a mile off. Besides, your perfume announces you."

"You should know," whispered the skunk, "that he's blind."

"But I'm not deaf," called the owl. "My hearing is keen. Make a note of it."

"Mr. Titus Pillowby Owl, may I present your new tenants, some rabbity mother or other, with two children in tow. The Watercress family, I think they're called."

Mr. Owl didn't bother to swivel his head. "Ah, yes. You've taken the basement lodgings. Rent is ten moths a night. Failure to pay on time means you forfeit either your rooms or yourselves. Luckily I'm not fond of bunny hash, but I might change my mind. Take it or leave it."

"That's outrageous!" said Cress's mother.

"In return," said the owl, "I will keep watch over your children. They will be safe. No one messes with me.

I promise not to abandon my post here. You can go scratch up whatever you need to make your son his medicinal tea. We worked this out already, didn't we?"

"You surely did," piped up a sleepy songbird in a nest. "I did the tweeting myself."

Mama peered into the single room. It was crammed into the roots of the oak. The carpet was too large. It rolled halfway up two opposite walls. But there was the rocker she'd sent on ahead, and the chipped teapot, and the portrait of Papa propped up on the dresser.

Mama fluted her voice skyward. "How do we catch the moths?"

"Light a candle," advised the owl. "Light a candle in the darkness. Moths can't resist a flame. They flutter near, get stuck in the wax, and die. It's sad but it happens, Ms. Watercress."

"Mrs. Watercress," she corrected him. "I had preferred being Ms., but with my husband so recently gone, it comforts me to use Mrs. for now."

"I'll bid my adieu," said Lady Cabbage. "If you change your mind and want to send your daughter off to a life of service in a fine home where she can learn some manners, send me word. Perhaps our paths will cross again."

The owl cleared his throat. "Bye-bye, Agatha Cabbage. Watch out for the Final Drainpipe."

"He had better watch out for me," she replied. Her chinchilla shivered.

A wind came up, a distant loon warbled with a lonely voice, and the Watercress family dove into their new digs.

As Mama fumbled for the box of matches, Cress said, "I could tell you didn't like that skunk."

Mama said, "I've never heard of any opera troupe in these woods. I don't trust folks who put on airs. Stay away from her, Cress. For your own good."

7

WOLVES WALKING THE WALLS

I t's not so bad, is it?" asked Mama, lighting a brass lantern.

Cress didn't answer.

"It's only one room," said Mama, "but doesn't that make it cozier?"

"Why did you bother bringing the drapes?" asked Cress. "There aren't even any windows except that narrow slit where the tree has split."

Mama sighed. "We'll want our privacy, living so close to other folks."

Cress turned her back on her mother.

Kip woke up and looked around. "Papa?" he murmured.

"We'll be safer here," said Mama. "Cress, help me unpack."

Kip crawled into the balls of yarn that spilled out of Mama's valise. When he had finished messing them up, he said again, "Papa!"

"This is our new home, Kip," said Mama. "Would you like a biscuit?"

"PAPA!"

Cress put some carrot juice in a sippy cup. That usually helped. But Kip threw the sippy cup out the door. He wailed.

"I hope that little monster settles down," said a voice from the doorway. "I live one flight up, and the walls are thin. I wouldn't like to have to file a complaint with the landlord on your first night. I'm the superintendent of this place."

In hobbled an elderly field mouse as if he had the perfect right to do so. He had a moustache and a cane. "He'll wake the whole building," said the mouse. "Mr. Owl is nocturnal, but at my age I need my zzzzzzz's. Simmer down, young pup. Get a grip."

"I'm sorry," said Mama. "He's overexcited. New things are scary for the very young."

"New things are scary for the elderly, too," said the mouse, "and he's the scariest baby I've ever seen."

"No BABY!" screamed Kip. Cress tried to pick him up, but he kicked her in the nose.

"Here, kid," said the mouse. "Want to see a face uglier than yours?"

Kip shifted one paw to see. Before the lantern, the mouse threw his shadow, making it seem like a ferocious wolf. "I used to do impressions on the circuit," he muttered to Mama. "The pay was lousy, but they kept you in corn."

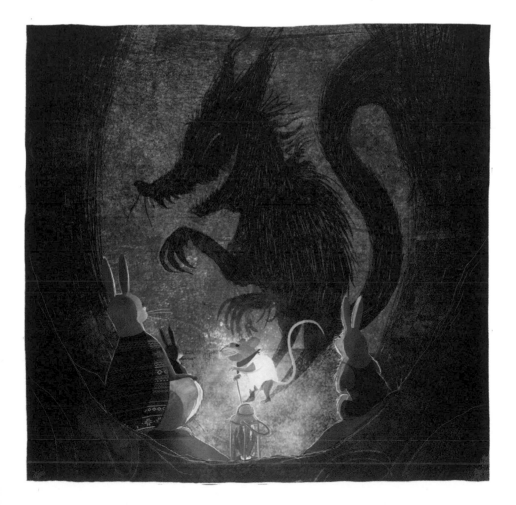

Cress thought that a wolf on the wall wasn't likely to comfort Kip, but her brother stopped wailing and said, "Do BUNNY."

The mouse made a shadow bunny, and a cow, and then a clot of spider in a sloppy web. No, that was a real spider in the corner. But when Kip asked for Rotty, the mouse was stumped. "My noggin's drawing a blank on that one," said the mouse. "What's a rotty?"

Mama was setting up her floor loom. Cress had an idea. She handed the stuffed carrot to the old mouse. He held it in front of the light. On the wall appeared a shadow carrot the size of a boulder. Kip giggled, grabbed his carrot and hugged it, and closed his eyes.

"That's better," said the mouse. "Now maybe the rest of us can get some shut-eye, too. I'll catch you in the morning, kiddos, and show you around."

"I can't thank you enough," said Mama.

"No, you can't," agreed the mouse. "But that's showbiz."

Cress saw the mouse to the door and stepped outside with him. He lit up a small cigar and took a puff, elegantly. The moon had sunk now and was swimming among the branches. "Where's it going?" asked Cress.

"It'll be back tomorrow. Don't you know that?" said the mouse. "Trust the moon. I'll be back tomorrow, too. Day by day and sun to moon, I'm your guy. But don't push it."

"Too much conversation down there," called the owl. "Make a note of it."

"Better be getting back to Sophie. That's my wife. She'll be wondering where I am. Mañana, kid." The field mouse scurried on his stiff old limbs to a knothole in the tree, just upstairs from the rabbits.

Cress looked in the ground-level shadows again, just in case Papa was there somehow. The shadows moved in the wind but stayed merely shadowy. Then Cress got scared and went back inside. She wanted to ask Mama what a circuit was and what "mañana" meant. But Mama was asleep in a heap of yarn.

Cress pulled a blanket over her and another one over Kip. She blew the candle out and lay awake in the dark. She saw wolves walking on all the walls.

8

WHERE WE WERE, REALLY

Kip was banging Cress over the head with Rotty. "Uppy, Cwessie," he cried.

"What a sleepy-ears you are," said her mother fondly. "Long trip last night. But breakfast is served on the lawn. Let's go."

Cress couldn't believe she'd slept, but sure enough, her eyes were sandy. She held still while her mother brushed her whiskers. "First impressions," said Mama. Then they hopped up into the shattering sunlight.

With the adventure of being out late last night, Cress had almost forgotten that the world wasn't just day and night. It was also seasonal. And this morning the world had decided to be spring.

Spring shows up with dash, even in a scary new neighborhood.

The Watercress family stood holding paws at the edge of the bluff upon which the old apartment tree perched. The drop was steep, but a track circled to a grassy patch below. Cress saw wild turkeys stalking in single file. A doe and her fawn tiptoed in slow motion, listening for trouble every few steps. Budding trees foamed with pale color.

Cress had hoped to find other rabbits. She'd had to say goodbye to her rabbit friends back home. She saw no rabbits yet. Everything else but. The tree was humming with morning business.

In the penthouse, perched on the broken-off top, Mr. Owl looked like part of the tree. Mangy and a little stout.

Below him, songbirds swooped, collecting flotsam for home improvement. Their nest balanced on a high limb.

Below them, a mother squirrel was doling out acorns to her four offspring, who swung their tails like furry pendulums. At this dawn hour, the mother looked weary already. The father squirrel chirruped to the rabbits below, "Welcome to the Broken Arms, you newbies."

"Why is this establishment named the Broken Arms?" called Mama.

The father squirrel gestured above his head.

Leafless and blistered by blight, the dead tree trunk had

split into two thick stems. Indeed, the forking trunk looked like someone raising his hands in the air above his head. Holding Mr. Titus Pillowby Owl upon an open palm.

This place sure isn't ready for a garden tour, thought Cress. Bugs were chewing away at the dead wood. Some evil-looking fungus ruffled out sideways here and there like a poison collar.

"You go get your num-nums," called the father squirrel to his new neighbors, "and we'll chat later."

From around the back of the tree appeared the old

mouse they'd met last night. He was helping his wife down the fire escape. He waved. "Oh, you. The day's ruined before it even got started," he said, but not in a mean way.

"Good morning to you, too," said Mama starchily.

"Don't mind me," said the mouse, inching along. "I'm a grouch because my wife has arthritis. So does my moustache. But welcome to the Broken Arms anyway, welcome to Hunter's Wood, welcome to a sad and sorry life with the likes of us."

"Let's stay positive," said Mama.

"This lovely lump of mouse is my wife," said the mouse. "Sophie. My name is Manfred Crabgrass. I'm Manny, or just the Man. I'm the super, and I got a super idea. You got a problem with your pipes, fix them yourself." He laughed at his own joke. Sophie rolled her eyes with wifely patience.

"I have to get these kits some breakfast," said Mama. "Later, dudes."

That didn't sound much like Mama, but Cress was willing to accept that Mama had some surprises in her yet.

They hopped down the winding path to the great lawn. The grass was so high that the Watercress family lost one another at first. "Stay close to me," said Mama.

They had only begun to nibble when a young squirrel voice called out, "Snake!" The rabbits froze, ready to explode into flight, but other boy-squirrel voices snickered.

"What've I told you about that!" cried the mother squirrel to her kits. "Sorry, everyone! False alarm!"

The super's voice was stern. "We've talked about this! One more time, Mrs. Oakleaf, and I'll evict your whole family! We have no patience for dangerous games like that."

"I hear ya, Manny. I'll deal with it," she replied. The squirrel parents hissed at their offspring. Everyone else went back to eating.

While finishing his breakfast, Kip lost Rotty somewhere. The Watercress family hunted in the tall grass until they found him. They stayed close together. Nearly touching. By the time they got back to the Broken Arms, the other residents had gone about their business. The buzzy world had turned down its volume a little.

Cress was cross to see that when they got safely back to their new place, it didn't feel like home yet. It still felt like a mistake.

"Papa?" asked Kip.

Mama pointed to the picture of Papa and turned to her yarns.

That's not going to work, thought Cress. Kip glanced at the portrait. He sat down with his back to it and began to suck on his carrot. He shot a look at Cress.

He mostly can't talk yet, thought Cress. But he knows.

9

What to Watch Out For

Kip was too young for cards, so they played hide-and-seek. But almost the only place to hide in a one-room apartment was under the flop-edge of the carpet, which was too easy.

Mama was all business, dressing her loom. When Kip fell into a nap while crouching under Mama's stringed canopy, Cress said, "I'm bored. I want to go out. Meet some rabbit friends."

"I can't take you out," said Mama. "And you know I can't leave Kip here alone."

Cress thought about how this was supposed to be working. "May I go play with the squirrel family, then?" she asked.

"Doctor Squirrel's family is out for the day," said Manfred, again in the doorway. What a busybody that mouse was. But maybe it was his job as super to check in on the new tenants. "The doctor had to give his youngsters a good talking-to about that Fake Snake game, and it's too public here for that kind of language. I can show Cress the ropes, if you want, Mrs. W."

"We don't really know you yet," said Mama from a tangle of colored threads.

"I don't know you yet, either," replied Manny. "But I see that the baby's napping. You should catch some shut-eye yourself while you can. Look, I've raised my litters. I know what I'm on about. Cut yourself some slack."

"Oh, well, then," said Mama, hiding a smile and then a yawn. "Not for long, though."

"We'll just take in the local scene. Back in a jiffy." Mr. Crabgrass hitched his thumbs in the armholes of his vest. "We'll be within hollering distance if you need us."

Manfred led Cress around the steep granite outcropping on which the Broken Arms stood. Behind, the hill sloped to a stream beneath a willow tree. Cress could see the forest beyond, frothed with confetti bud. And beyond that? An orangey finger pointing at the sky. Another next to it. "What kind of tree is that?" she asked.

"Ah, that's a pair of chimneys," said the mouse. "We don't hopscotch that far, kiddo. Danger that way."

"What kind of animal builds chimneys that tall? A bear?"

"Ah, you want to talk bears?" Manfred turned Cress away from the forest and the far chimneys. "Has anyone told you about Tunk the Honeybear?"

Cress shook her head. So Manfred said, "Let me tell you what to avoid around here. First, there's the Final Drainpipe. That old snake usually lives upslope under some sunning rocks. But he is one shifty menace. Fact is, he could turn up underfoot anywhere. So watch out."

Cress said, "Lady Cabbage already told us about the snake."

"Second," said Manny, "there's Tunk the Honeybear. He'll be your competition for honey. He's been stung by bees so often, he's gone a bit off. He's not mean, but sometimes he has these notions, like? They come on all at once. Usually everyone runs. You know how to run?"

"Excuse me," said Cress. "I'm a *rabbit*."

"Then, third—" Manfred Crabgrass looked over his shoulder back at the forest. "Beyond Hunter's Wood? Down the cliffs? The chimneys? That's just the start of it. It's a war zone over there. Makes hereabouts look like the Happy Acres petting zoo. So don't go there and don't let your Mama go there and don't let Kip go there."

"A war zone? I don't know what you mean," said Cress.

"You don't want to know," said the mouse. But he was wrong. Cress did want to know.

They had made a loop and were turning around. "Oh, one other thing," said Cress. "Are there any other rabbit families around?"

"Not anymore," said the super.

10

THE OAKLEAF FAMILY

W as it Reynard the fox?" asked Cress. "I mean, why there are no other rabbits?"

"Can't say for sure," said Manfred. "We used to have a population, but they got the jitters and skedaddled. We try to look out for one another, but things happen. Life scrabbles on, good and bad together."

At the Broken Arms, they heard a ruckus of squirrels. "Oh, goody, the little scholars are back," said the super. He added, "Hey, kid. Take care of your mama. She's going through a rough patch."

Inside, Mama was pouring thimbles of lemonade for the mother squirrel. The four squirrel kits were playing a game that only had one rule: bite a tail. They ran around biting one another's tails. Kip screamed with joy and wanted to play until his tail got bit. Then he screamed for lack of joy.

"So sorry," said the mother squirrel. "They should go outside. Kids, go outside. Are you paying attention? The little monsters never pay attention. Brewster! Finian! Teddy! Jo-Jo! Outside! And no playing Fake Snake." Brewster, Finian, Teddy, and Jo-Jo darted outside, biting as they went.

"You're okay with them outdoors on their own?" asked Mama. "I mean, what with that snake business?"

"They're not on their own—they're all together," said the mother squirrel. "Hello, little missy. What are you called?"

"That's Cressida," said her mother. "Cress, this is Lolly Oakleaf."

Cress didn't want to stay inside, all old-lady–like. But she also didn't want to go outside and get her tail bit. "I'll wind the warps for you, Mama," she said.

"Cress is such a comfort," said Mama to Mrs. Oakleaf. To Cress she said, "I'm going with spring colors, sweetie. Moss green and fern with a touch of bronze for glint. Four, four, and two. Want me to count it out for you?"

Cress shook her head. She had done this before. Winding a warp meant collecting the colors in the right order and not making mistakes. So she arranged the balls of yarn. She found the leading thread on each ball and began to pull.

When the warp was ready, Mama would thread its organized colors through the heddles of the floor loom. Then she would step on one of the pedals. Each pedal plucked and raised a separate set of strings. While certain strings were hoisted, Mama would shoot the correct color of cross thread through them using one of several shuttles. She'd press the cross threads, the weft, tight with a beater. Making cloth appear inch by inch—making patterns in cloth appear—seemed magical to Cress no matter how many times she watched it happen. She wished she could make things, too.

Kip was sitting on his mother's lap and sucking on Rotty. Mrs. Oakleaf filled Cress's mother in on the local gossip.

"Mustn't be late with the rent," said the mother squirrel. "We live in dread of being evicted. Or being lunch. Not that I've ever known Mr. Owl to eat a tenant, but there's always a first time. He can be fierce!"

"I can hear you down there," called Mr. Owl. His voice carried right into the apartment. "Make a note of it."

"He's very distinguished. Very fine sense of hearing. Also a little nosy," said Mrs. Oakleaf in a theatrical voice. She meant to be heard. But Mama got up and quietly closed the door.

Mrs. Oakleaf rolled her eyes. "So, Mr. Owl roosts in the penthouse. Now, the songbirds who live one level down are the eyes of the neighborhood. They see everything and broadcast it."

Cress walked the threads back and forth, looping them around the winding pegs that Mama had hung on the wall. Kip sulked.

"Below the songbirds, that's us Oakleafs," said the squirrel mother. "A spot of bother to one and all. Into each life a little nuttiness must fall, and that's us. Dr. Oakleaf is out most days. He makes house calls. I'm stuck at home with this litter of rascals. Below us, you have Manny and Sophie Crabgrass, whom you've met. Last, you in the basement flat. Where did you come from?"

Cress thought, We came from yesterday.

Mama said something vague and changed the subject.

"What about other rabbits?" asked Cress after a while.

"Rabbits run," said Lolly Oakleaf. "Folks move on. It's nature's way. I do hope you'll stay, though."

After Lolly Oakleaf had left, after dinner in the slanting light of sunset, Mama lit a wax candle. She put it in the doorsill. The three rabbits sat close to one another on a root outside their door.

Drawn by the light, a few moths came fluttering by. They got stuck in the wet wax and perished. Mama picked them out using a pair of knitting needles as if they were chopsticks. "What a messy life," she said, nearly to herself. "Ghastly, really. Bring me a dish, Cress."

Cress held the dish and wrinkled her nose in distaste as they counted moths. "This doesn't seem fair," said Cress.

"Tell me what's fair in life," replied her mother. That was a question that didn't seem to have an answer tonight.

Cress pointed out the moon rising. It was almost the same size as last night, but seemed to have put on a little weight. "Look, it's growing. It must have eaten some stars for breakfast."

Her mother said, abstractly, "The celestial sciences are too far above me. But stars grow back, you know, when they're eaten. Like grass."

"Do moths grow back?" asked Cress.

"Not moths."

"Mama," said Cress, "do you realize that this whole day is a day that Papa knows nothing about? He doesn't know about the Broken Arms or all these new neighbors. He can't know about what's happened to us since we left home."

"Sweetie-cakes," said Mama, "I do realize that. Indeed I do. But we have to keep on. We have to pay our rent. We have to watch out for enemies. We have to take care of Kip. We have work to do."

From above, the voice of Mr. Owl floated down. It had a lullaby tone for such a gruff old bird. "Why don't you go inside now? I think you all need a snuggle. I can wait for the rent till tomorrow. Tomorrow's good enough."

"Tomorrow's good enough," repeated Mama in a whispery voice, winking at Cress and patting Kip on the soft spot between his ears. Not a promise. Just a hope. Maybe tomorrow couldn't be good, but maybe it could be good enough.

11

SNOW ALERT

The next day they had breakfast in a soft shower.

Cress liked to eat in the rain. Rain gave cover against birds of prey, and it made the grass taste fresher. Unless it splashed dirt up in the grass. Who likes dirt in their breakfast? Nobody except worms.

A second day of rain. One of the squirrel kits started to play Fake Snake, but his brothers bit him to make him stop.

Then a third rainy day after that. It was spring—what do you expect?

But the following morning: surprise. Snow made a comeback. Mama baked some cheese popovers for a treat.

The squirrel kits came by to play with Cress and Kip, but they were too wild. They bounced on the warp threads of Mama's loom. Threads tore. Mama had to complain to their mother.

Oh, but were those kits in trouble. Lolly Oakleaf threw them outside in the snow. "Every last one of you, you hear? The nerve! I should bite all your tails." The kits had to babysit Kip to make up for being such a bother to Mrs. Watercress.

Mama murmured to Cress, "That Lolly Oakleaf has lost control of her children."

After lunch the super showed up, as usual. It was his job to carry the daily rent upstairs to Mr. Owl, since rabbits don't climb trees and Mr. Owl never deigned to come down.

Mama handed over the dead moths pressed in a paper napkin. "What does he do with them?" she asked in a low voice.

"My guess is: breakfast, lunch, supper, and midnight snack," said Manfred Crabgrass.

"How are we to find moths today?" asked Mama. "Moths don't fly during a snowstorm. I don't want to fall behind on my rent."

"No, you don't," Manny agreed. He regarded the spiderweb on the ceiling. "Sometimes you can pick up a spare moth in a spiderweb, if you get to it before

Señorita Spider does," he said. But today the web was empty of moths.

Cress was tired of hearing about Mama's worries. She was a kid. She could take only so much. "I'm going to play with the boys," she said. Without waiting for permission, she went out.

Only one squirrel was there, with Kip. They were rolling snowballs. "Where are your brothers?" asked Cress.

"They got bored," said the squirrel. "They went to the riverbank to ring the old possum's doorbell. They all hide when he answers it."

"Why aren't you with them?" asked Cress.

"I didn't want to leave this little fellow alone out here," he replied, indicating Kip. "Monsieur Reynard is as hungry on snowy days as on sunny ones."

"Oh." Cress squinted at him. "Which brother are you?"

"I'm Finny," said the squirrel.

Cress helped Finny and Kip make snowballs. Then they rolled Kip into his own snow cocoon. He laughed and laughed. "Finny funny," he said more than once, as if the saying was the funny part.

"How do your parents find moths for Mr. Owl when it is snowing out?" asked Cress. Nosy of her, she knew, but it was hard to keep having fun while there was worrying to be done.

"I think we pay in acorns," said Finny. "I don't know. That's grown-up stuff."

"I can hear you," Mr. Owl reminded them. A hooty voice through the snow.

Cress got the idea to make snow moths. They lay down in the fluff and moved their limbs to scrape out wing patterns. "Can you take today's rent in snow moths?" called Cress.

"I rarely eat snow for dinner," replied Mr. Owl. Then his voice changed. "Inside at once! On the double!" he barked, all business.

Finian's brothers came pelting along from the direction of the riverbank. "Fox alert!" they cried. "Monsieur Reynard!" Their voices were more urgent than when they played Fake Snake.

The youngsters all ducked into the Watercress apartment because it was nearest. They kept very still. Mama gave Kip a caramel to busy his mouth.

They peered through the doorway. Monsieur Reynard was picking his way through the snow, a red paintbrush stroking sideways against nubbly white snow-paper. His nose was down and his eyes were slits. He meant business.

He studied the snow moths, sniffed, and glanced around with a wily look.

BAM! A big clot of snow on his head. "Bull's-eye!" cried Mr. Owl.

Monsieur Reynard left the neighborhood at a gallop.

"Yay," shouted the rowdy Oakleaf boys, and Cress, too. Kip's mouth was too stuck with caramel to be able to join in.

12

PLANNING A HEIST

A few days after the ambush by snow, spring came back, this time with conviction.

Almost everyone from the Broken Arms went out to bask in the sun. They joined neighbors from nearby nests and hidey-holes. It was a frolic, like a country fair.

The super helped his wife to the stream, which had become noisy with snow melt. On her stiff hips, Sophie lowered herself to soak her bunions. She hummed tunelessly.

Clouds of new-hatched midges swarmed the air like silver dust. The songbirds ate so much, their stomachs hurt. Then they sang songs about the joys of gluttony.

Yes, yes, a hundred yesses. The world was weaving itself back together after a long winter. Green threads running in all directions, and color splashes for contrast. Wild purple crocuses unfurled, and junior daffodils.

The squirrel brothers played hide-and-seek amidst the new foliage of birches. Cress wished she could climb up there and see what it was like for herself.

Even Mama showed up for the fun. She brought a blanket to sit on and a flask of mint chocolate. After the snack, Kip played Hide the Rotty with Cress. Then he found a mud puddle, so he played Hide the Rotty in Mud, all by himself.

Coming down to earth, Finian scampered by. He was full of news from higher up and farther off. "The honeybees are awake," he said. "So Tunk the Honeybear will be awake soon, too, I bet."

"Oh, really?" Mama looked up from her knitting. "I'm almost out of last season's supply. I'd better make a run tonight before this Tunk tiptoes off with whatever honey there is. Kip hasn't been short of breath lately, but he's due for an attack once pollen season hits."

"You don't want to meet Tunk the Honeybear when he's in a mood," said Finny. "He can be a bruiser when he gets stung by bees." In a bossy, landlordy voice, he added, "Make a note of it."

"I heard that," called Mr. Owl from his penthouse. "Make a note of it."

"Did you see any other rabbits?" Cress asked Finny, but he had run off.

"Mr. Owl, why don't you come down and join us?" called Mama. "We have enough mint chocolate to share, and some carrot cake."

"I don't socialize with tenants," said Mr. Owl. He turned

his head around on his neck so it was facing the other direction. Kip stuck out his tongue. "I heard that," said Mr. Owl.

The day seemed to unfold like a pleated fan, becoming ever richer with spring scent. Oh, if only Papa were here, it would be perfect, thought Cress. She sighed. Mama looked up sharply but said nothing. She just pursed her lips and clicked her knitting needles.

Manfred Crabgrass ambled over with a cigar. "Did I hear you say you were going to harvest some honey? This early in the season? You'll be lucky to get a single teaspoon of the new batch."

"A single teaspoon is worth the effort, if it's on hand when it's needed," said Mama. "But my husband used to do this. I don't know how to go about it."

"Bring some wax to put in your ears," suggested Manny. "The honeybees are quietest at night, but if they drone in their sleep, it can get on your nerves. You have to be quick. In and out, like a master thief. That way you won't get stung the way Tunk the Honeybear does. He usually works in broad daylight. He's noisy and bullying, and the bees don't like it."

"Thanks for the tip," said Mama, examining her knitting.

"I'll mind the kids when you go," Manny offered. "I'll

make them do push-ups and times tables and clean their rooms."

"We only have one room," Mama reminded the mouse.

The super would come downstairs after supper. He promised not to smoke inside because of Kip's weak lungs. Mama planned to leave by the light of the rising moon.

"Do you really think you should go alone?" asked Cress. She hated the thought of having Mama disappear at night by herself the way Papa had done.

But then Kip popped up. "Kip SWIMMY," said Kip proudly. He had been diving for Rotty in the mud puddle. Mama put Cress's question aside for a washcloth and scrub brush.

Kip's screams silenced the songbirds. Old Manny and Sophie hobbled back inside and slammed their door.

"Do you really think you should go all alone?" asked Cress again.

Mama didn't answer.

"Mama, what do you think happened to all the other rabbits?" asked Cress.

Mama was busy rummaging through her things for a scarf. Again she didn't answer.

13

THE HIVE AND THE HONEY

They had an early dinner of baby violets served on a bed of lawn.

Manfred Crabgrass had run a footbath for his wife before coming downstairs. "I had to play a couple of rounds of poker with her before I could leave. My buttercup plays to win. She's a shark. But then, she's always had a wild streak. You wouldn't know it, what with the bad hip and the blood pressure."

"I'll be back with a beaker of fresh honey as soon as I can," said Mama. She put on her kerchief and some black gloves. She looked like a jewel thief. Cress didn't have a good feeling about this caper.

After kissing Cress and Kip, Mama darted outside. She shot glances this way and that. Then she disappeared, a rabbit on a mission.

Manny began to play pat-a-cake with Kip. Cress felt torn, like a worm that is bitten in half but goes on wriggling in two pieces. Finally she cried, "Oh, Mama forgot her map again!" and, without any map, dashed out the door before Manny could utter a word.

He managed to utter quite a few words from the doorway, however. They weren't from anyone's list of polite words.

But Cress kept on. She could smell her mother's warm haste brushed here and there against the green world. Cress followed as quickly as she could. When she got to an open patch of moss, the sort of place where deer like to pose and look noble, she saw Mama on the far side.

Above the clearing bloomed the moon again. It seemed a fatter lantern than before. It was thriving on the spring.

Finian Oakleaf had told Mama how to find the tree with the beehive. And there it was. On the far side of the mossy dell, a hemlock drooped its weary arms to the forest floor. Just where the largest limb met the trunk of the tree, a knothole gaped. It looked to Cress like the secret lung of the tree. She could hear it softly breathing. What if those bees had trapped Papa in there and were holding him for ransom?

Cress watched from the shadows. Her mama stopped, pulled two plugs of wax from her apron pocket, and fixed them in her ears. Then Mama took a step on the sloping branch that rose to the beehive.

For how long had Cress wanted to climb a tree? But rabbits don't climb trees. They haven't the cling for it. What luck that the bees had built their hive at the end of a convenient runway.

Mama was climbing too slowly. They're going to wake up any minute and tell you to buzz off, thought Cress. Mama, hurry up!

Then Cress felt her whiskers freeze. She turned.

Into the mossy clearing lurched a hillock of rank fur.

Tunk the Honeybear, awake from his winter sleep and hungry for breakfast by moonlight. At least Cress guessed it was Tunk. Who else could smell like a season's worth of must and damp? He crossed the grassy floor on all fours, sniffing the aromas of new growth and new scat. Checking it all out. His head was down. He hadn't seen Cress yet.

"Mama," hissed Cress in a whisper. She didn't dare call louder—she might alert the bear. She might wake the bees. But Mama's ears were stuffed with wax. She didn't hear Cress.

So Cress just stood on the apron of the fringy branch of hemlock up which her mother had climbed so timidly.

"You'll have to stop right here," she said in the smallest possible voice when Tunk's nose had come within a couple of yards of her station.

The bear's nose rose, and the rest of his head followed. "What have we here?" he murmured. His eyes were masked with meanness. He squinted. Maybe he needed glasses. "Is this some spirit of the forest dressed up in bunny pajamas?"

"As a matter of fact, yes," said Cress, trying to go with the flow. "You nailed it in one. That's me. I'm, um, a woodland spirit. This is my territory. I'm the boss. Move along now—nothing to see here."

Tunk began to stand up. He was a mountain. The stink was atrocious—like a walking dump heap. Fringed epaulets capped his shoulders. Around his boulder of a neck he wore a necklace made of dead bees strung together.

"Move aside," he growled. "I have a reservation."

"Not to be rude first thing in the springtime," whispered Cress, "but you reek to high heaven. Go have a bath and come back later."

"I always start my year with a gargle of honey," replied Tunk. "It gets the juices rolling and puts hair on my chest. Enough small talk." He reached out a massive paw to bat Cress away.

"Touch me and I'll scream, and the bees will come to my rescue," she warned. "You think I'm joking? I really am the spirit of the forest."

"I string dead bees for a hobby!" he reminded her. "Trophies." But he dropped his paw and inched closer. His face softened. In a humbler voice, he said, "If you truly are the spirit of the vales and vapors, what is your game? Why are you appearing to me?"

"I want to know," she said, to buy time and also to hear what he would say. "Did you attack my father?"

"As a rule, I don't eat bunny chops," he replied. "Though I might step on a passerby if one got in my way. I'm not as mean as they say, but I'm not nimble, either. I got a big chassis that's hard to steer."

"I need to find out," she said. "Papa went missing a short while ago, and he's never come home."

"Honey-bunny," he said, which sounds rude until you remember that he was talking to a young rabbit at the foot of a beehive. "I just woke up from my long winter's nap. I haven't been out making the rounds yet. I didn't come across any daddy rabbit."

Just then Mama backed her tail out of the knothole in the hemlock tree. When she turned around and saw Cress on the ground staring a slab of bear in the eye, Mama didn't shriek and she didn't faint. She only took the wax plugs out of her ears and said, "I'm sorry. I was busy in the back room. How may we help you?"

"Lady," he said, "I have a rendezvous with a little honey I know."

"Very little, I'm afraid," she said. "I've been inspecting the supplies. But help yourself. We were just leaving." Mama's tone of voice was cold. She slid clumsily down the limb and took Cress by the paw. "As for you, missy, we'll discuss this at home. You move your tail now."

"Goodbye, Mr. Tunk," said Cress. "Thank you for not killing my father."

"What are you talking about?" asked Mama in a rage. Then they were away at a speed that few but rabbits can manage. True, Tunk was interested in honey, not rabbits. But Mama had already nipped what little output the bee factory had made so far this season. In a moment or two, the bear might not be so charmed by the furry spirit of the woodland and her mother.

14

GROUNDED

Back at the Broken Arms, Mama let loose at Cress. Manny joined in. There were four of "How dare you" and several of "If I ever catch you again" and about a half dozen of that old favorite, "What were you thinking? You weren't thinking!" Mama and Manny wrapped it up with a final chorus of "How dare you?" A duet of outrage. As if they'd been practicing for days.

Kip slept through the whole shebang, kicking his little feet in the air.

Manny fixed Mama a cup of mint tea. When Mama paused to take the first sip, Cress squeezed a word in. "But honestly! What would you have done if I hadn't followed you, Mama? You didn't hear Tunk approaching because your ears were full of wax. He might have awakened all the bees, and they would have stung you. Or he might have accidentally knocked you to the ground and broken your neck."

Mama's mouth was full of tea, so Cress went on. "I'm not a little kid anymore! If you'd gotten Tunked, what would have happened to Kip? I can't raise a baby!"

"Don't speak to your mother like that," said Manny. "She can't take it. And I was worried sick, too, you know. I had a bad attack of bonkus of the konkus."

"Mama, if you'd gone with Papa that night and kept a lookout for him," said Cress, throwing it all out there, "maybe Papa wouldn't have gotten, whatever. Dead."

"Oh, my," said Manny in a small voice, "there's my ride. I'm outta here, folks. Mañana." He closed the door behind him so softly that there was no click of the latch.

Mama began to weep. She didn't have another room she could escape to, so she crawled into the flap-over of the carpet to muffle her tears.

Cress felt wicked and cross and proud of it, because she believed what she had said. "I mean, really," she declared. "What were you thinking?" But this sounded false. She'd gone too far. She'd made her mother cry. She wasn't proud of that. She wished Mama would stop.

"Come out, Mama," she said. "Look at the good-enough part. Nobody got hurt tonight. And you scored enough honey to tide us over till the bees step up production. Which they will when it gets warmer."

"I'm sleeping here tonight," called Mama, sniffling. "And you are so, so, so grounded that your new best friend can be dirt."

Cress stole Rotty from Kip's grasp and hugged it as she tried to sleep, thinking, We live in a hole in the ground. How much more grounded can I be?

But she found out.

The next day Dr. Oakleaf was taking his family to the raspberry patch for a picnic. They asked Cress and Kip to join them.

"Don't even think about it," said Mama in a cold voice behind her.

Kip came home painted red with raspberry ink.

The day after that it was rainy. Kip had caught a cold. He needed honey-ginger tea for his breathing. He slept all day, which was peaceful in a wheezy sort of way.

Cress helped Mama thread the floor loom. She wasn't good at it because her paws weren't as deft as Mama's. "What pattern are you going to work on today?" she asked.

Cress could tell that Mama wasn't ready to be normal but was getting tired of being frosty. Being frosty was hard work. "I was thinking," said Mama, "against long panels of red and gold background, I might weave in some pale blue and grey moths."

"Yuck," said Cress politely. "Gross."

"Well," said Mama, "like it or not, we harvest moths to pay the rent. And sooner or later, moths do eat my work, after all. Moths like wool. So picturing them seems only fair. I mean given that nothing about this life is fair."

"Tell me about it," said Cress.

"Don't start," said her mother. So Cress didn't.

The third day Doctor Squirrel and Finian showed up at

the doorway. Mama took a dim view of others butting into her affairs. "She's not ready for release yet," said Mama.

"You know best," said the doctor. "I just thought Cress might be driving you crazy, underfoot all day. Look, I brought these small pads of paper. I use them to write prescriptions on. Our Finian said that your Cress might like them to draw on. They're extras."

He handed over three pads of paper that were shaped like white cubes. Some sticky stuff made one edge adhere. You could draw on the top sheet, lift the other edge like the page of a book, and gently pull. The whole thing would come off. A separate piece of white paper about three inches square.

"Where did you get these?" asked Cress. She'd never seen anything like them before.

"In my little black bag of doctor's supplies," said Dr. Oakleaf, winking.

"As long as you're here, I wonder if you'd glance at our Kip," asked Mama.

Dr. Oakleaf looked at Kip and said, "Keep him in honey-ginger tea when the catarrh flares up. He'll outgrow this. He's just a little bunny."

"BIG," said Kip croakily.

"Mrs. Watercress, when does Cress get out of prison?" Finian asked.

"Maybe tomorrow. If she's good," said Mama. "We'll see."

"I hope so. We're going out on our raft tomorrow. The stream is running high."

"I said, Finian, that we'll see," said Mama. Cress knew that meant "Yes, but I'm not saying so yet." Then Mama turned to the doctor. "Thank you, Doctor. You were kind to look Kip over."

"Plenty of rest and drink lots of water," said the doctor as he left. "You, too. Mothers have to keep up their strength."

Cress let Kip have one cube of the paper. He sat there and pulled off all the pages until he was covered in sticky white squares. He looked like a shaggy paper monster.

"More," he said.

"The rest are mine," said Cress. But she didn't know what she would do with them.

Kip sneezed, and a paper blizzard crossed the room and stuck to Mama. Even she laughed a little. So, phew, the anger season was just about over.

15

ON THE HIGH SEAS

Tell me," said Mama, "about this raft business."

"Oh, it's safer than houses," said Mrs. Oakleaf. "Hardly any of our kids have ever drowned."

Mama gave her a look.

"Just kidding. Joke!" said Lolly Oakleaf.

"Not a funny joke," replied Mama.

"Seriously," continued Lolly Oakleaf, "if it were dangerous, would I let them go? I ask you."

"You do have four of them," said Mama. "You could afford to lose one or two."

Lolly Oakleaf gave Mama a look.

"Joke!" said Mama blandly.

The raft could only hold five passengers, so Kip wasn't

invited. "You can't come. You have to stay home and babysit Rotty," said Cress. She was eager to break out of the tiny flat and go off with the squirrels.

"HATE Rotty!" said Kip in a tone that didn't sound like: Joke!

The Oakleaf family carried oats and raisins in kerchiefs tied to the end of sticks. Like hobo squirrels. The boy squirrels hit one another with their lunches. A beanbag fight, of sorts. They didn't hit Cress.

Oddly, this made her feel left out.

Where the stream ran by the Broken Arms, it was only a trickle from a leaky faucet. A beetle could pop over it without wetting its feet. In fact, several beetles were practicing

their jumping from bank to bank. But beyond the willow tree, the stream broadened into a pond.

"Ah, the Good Ship *Jaffa*," said Dr. Oakleaf. He tugged an all-weather cover of woven grasses to reveal a shallow box. It had four sides and a bottom, no lid. The Oakleafs flipped it so its bottom was up, like a table. Made of pale balsa wood, the trim little raft smelled of oranges.

Brewster, Finian, Teddy, and Jo-Jo heaved it into the water. There was just enough room for one brother to hunch in each corner of the floating platform if Cress stood in the middle. She was fine keeping company with the heap of lunches. She was scared of water. She didn't know how to swim.

"Here's your emergency whistle." Dr. Oakleaf handed Brewster a little silver plug on a chain. Brewster put the chain on his neck and blew on the whistle to check its pitch. The doctor said, "Use it if you're in trouble, and we'll come. No playing that Fake Snake game, or you'll be sorry."

"Don't be worried, Cress," said Lolly Oakleaf "The pond is shallow. You could wade to shore if you wanted. Have a good trip, my fine buckaroos. Bon voyage!"

The sailors waved goodbye to the parents on the sunny shore. Dr. Oakleaf put a newspaper over his face and instantly began to snore. His wife wandered about, picking dandelion greens for supper.

"Let's be pirates and make Cress walk the plank," said Teddy.

"Walk your own plank," said Cress. "I don't do planks."

Finny said quickly, "Look: a wild jungle." He pointed to some reeds on the far bank. "Ferocious attack butterflies. Our lives will be in peril. Let's go explore."

"Cool," said everyone. All four squirrels began paddling at the four corners of the Good Ship *Jaffa*. But since they were all using their tails as rudders, the raft only went in circles.

"I feel dizzy. Or maybe seasick," said Cress.

"The wild jungle idea sucks. Let's get marooned on a desert island instead," said Jo-Jo.

But there weren't any desert islands in the pond.

"How about we go to the other end and see if we can spot salmon leaping upstream to spawn?" asked Brewster. "Maybe Tunk the Honeybear will be trying to snatch some sushi out of the air."

Cress didn't mention she'd already met Tunk, who had taken her for the spirit of the forest or something. Was that real for him or just pretend? Whatever, she didn't want a rendezvous with the bear.

The current of the pond lazed the raft around a bend. Out of sight of the Oakleaf parents, soon they were deep in no-squirrel's-land. Except for them. Vines trailed from overarching trees. They thought they could hear gorillas, or maybe dinosaurs.

Once Cress thought she saw a rabbit nose twitching from behind some fiddlehead ferns, but when she rubbed her eyes, it was gone.

Fetching up at the other end of the pond, the explorers peered over the break, looking for leaping salmon. The pond had been formed by a dam of small boulders. Water spilled over as if from an overfilled bathtub. In a trickle, the stream continued, dropping deeper into the woods, home of gloom and mystery and probably murderers.

"Let's have our lunches here," said Teddy. "Less to

carry when we paddle back." So the squirrels scrabbled for their sacks, disagreeing over who got the largest one.

"It doesn't matter: we're sharing with Cress, anyway," said Finny. But the squabble turned into roughhouse, with whacking sticks and the pulling of tails. When one of the lunch-bag poles caught the chain of the emergency whistle, the whistle went pinging through the air. It dropped in the water at the dam's edge.

"Now look what you've done," said Cress. "If we get attacked by wild butterflies or gorillas, we can't call your folks for help."

"You sound like our mom," said Jo-Jo in a way that didn't sound like a compliment.

Finny peered into the green water. "We'll get it. I can see the chain." He fished around with his paw but couldn't snag the chain. So Jo-Jo jumped in, and then Teddy and Brewster. More pushing and fighting.

At last one of them caught the edge of the chain and handed the loop to Finny, who pulled and pulled. But the whistle had gotten wedged in a crack between some rocks. They couldn't dislodge it.

Brewster reached for the pole from his lunch bag. "If we pry this rock up, Finny can pull the whistle loose," he said. He leaned on the pole to use it as a lever. The whistle was still stuck. "I can feel the boulder budging a little. Come on, guys, more weight on this end," said Brewster.

Up to their shoulders in the shallow water, the three squirrels threw their wet weight on the pole. The stick snapped, but not before the boulder shifted. The whistle came free. Finny fell backward on the raft, nearly knocking Cress overboard.

The boulder didn't settle back where it had been but rolled right over the edge of the dam. With echoing thuds, it bounded below. The pond, surprised at the change of architecture, lunged forcefully into the breach.

Before anyone could shout "Yikes!" or "Help!" the whole dam had given way. What had been a trickle became a waterfall. The Good Ship *Jaffa* surged ahead, with only Finny and Cress on board to tell the tale.

16

CASTAWAYS

The waterfall was a tilting shelf of water. Along the top slid the Good Ship *Jaffa*. It paused, as if sorry it had started out on this trip at all. Then it teetered and went over. Down, down. The torrent gulped at Finny and Cress as they fell. The noise was like hurricanes.

Cress got ready to be smashed on the rocks. But the streambed below gathered the flood in a basin and sent it churning forward, an unleashed whitewater frenzy.

Finny was hanging on with all the squirrely strength in his claws. His eyes were glazed with fear.

Without claws like Finny's, Cress lay on the raft with her arms stretched wide. Her jaws were clamped on the bitter wire that strung together the panels of the Good Ship *Jaffa*. Holding on by strength of will and overbite, she couldn't utter a word.

Whipped in a whirlpool, the vessel spun. Sometimes Finny and Cress went face-first into the white rapids ahead of them. Other times they were looking back up the cataract, the way they'd come.

No sight of Brewster, Teddy, or Jo-Jo up there. The stream plunged down many stony steps, caromed around many bends. Uncharted territory, for real.

Then, as the Good Ship *Jaffa* slowed in a calming eddy, Finny and Cress spotted more trouble. That bear with dead bees around his neck. He was hip-deep in the water, swiping for fish.

Cress knew she had to take charge. She loosened her jaw and her bite. Pulling herself to a sitting position, she called, "Hi, Tunk!"

Tunk the Honeybear swung around. "It's the spirit of the woodland!" he said. "Always showing up to provide guidance. Wearing bunny pajamas again. It must be all the rage this season. And who is that with you? Some magical helper?"

Finian sat up, too. "Yeah, right," he said. "I'm a Squirrel Scout earning a merit badge. Don't get too close or I'll have to bite your paw. And I might have rabies, you know. It happens."

Tunk drew his paw back as if afraid that Finny had

germs. "Actually, O Spirit, I was more interested in salmon than squirrel."

"Salmon it shall be," called Cress. "Let us pass without delay, and we'll float along and get right on it. I'll tell the salmon downstream that you're planning to have them for lunch sooner or later."

Perhaps Tunk is nearsighted, thought Cress. Or maybe he isn't very bright. Here we go. He's letting us drift by, out of his reach.

"That was clever of you," said Finny when they were out of Tunk's reach and also his hearing.

"Our paths have crossed before, Tunk's and mine," admitted Cress. She felt a little proud of that. "Is he a bit dim?"

"Dim is dim," said Finny, "but strong is bigger than dim. Maybe sometimes bigger *because* dim."

"Well, we escaped," said Cress. She let out a breath of relief. Too soon, because just then the Good Ship *Jaffa* plunged over an even steeper waterfall they hadn't seen coming.

They seemed to drop for several horrible lifetimes. When the vessel landed, it splintered apart. Cress and Finny went hurling face-first into the brink. Just in time Cress remembered to close her mouth. She didn't want to become a bunny with braces.

Drenched and shaken, they clambered up the bank. The battered shakes of balsa wood escaped downstream. One of them had the word JAFFA stenciled on it. Cress wished she could have saved that piece as a souvenir. She'd wanted to try writing that word on her small white paper pad: "The Shipwreck of the *Jaffa*: A Tale of Survival." If they survived.

"Now we're lost," said Finny. "What next?"

"Rescue," said Cress. "Why don't you blow your whistle and see if your parents come?"

Amazingly, the whistle was still around Finny's neck. But he shook his head. "We're too far for them to hear. Besides, we might alert some local menace to our whereabouts. Better move ahead quietly."

"Well, we can't climb up that cliff," said Cress. She pointed up the sheer rock face over which they'd plunged on the curtain of water.

Finny said, "We'll hack our way through the jungle and try to find a path up to the tableland where we started."

"What will we hack with?" asked Cress. "We don't have hatchets."

Finny smiled, showing his big brazen teeth. Cress smiled back. Their smiles were well matched. Perfect for jungle exploration.

17

MIDNIGHT INVITATION

They wandered for hours. The forest teased them with useless paths, sending them yonder and thither. Clouds had rolled in. The friends couldn't tell which way the sun was setting. They didn't know if they were getting more lost with every step.

How to manage being scared? They couldn't hold paws—that would be too awkward. So they each took one end of the chain. The whistle dangled between them silently.

"I bet it's going to rain," said Finny.

"I'm going to get in so much trouble that my mother might say some bad words," said Cress. "I'll be grounded until I'm a teenager."

"It is—it's starting to rain," said Finny. "I knew it."

"Why do things like this happen to rabbits?" asked Cress. "First my father, now me. It rains on the wretched."

"It's raining on me, too," Finny pointed out. "I'm not wretched. Just wet."

Cress said, "Is the world set up just to catch us? Is that what it's for?"

"I wish we had an umbrella. Squirrels don't really like the rain."

"Everywhere, dangers!" Cress was working herself into a state. "Why do I bother? Snakes and bears and whatever next around the corner?"

Finny said, "Let's take cover under that fallen log."

The space smelled of slugs and leaf mold. Once settled, Cress fell into a silence that had something granite in it, as if she had become a statue of herself. Like a cemetery statue put up after she had died, one she was buried below. Something that couldn't be scared because it was inert.

But statues couldn't hear, and she could. Finny was still talking. She wished he would shut up now.

"The thing is," said Finny, "we have to get back. It doesn't matter how long it takes. Cress, look at me."

Cress didn't want to look at him. She was a stone. She missed her mama and her papa, but she couldn't bear to show it.

"Cress," said Finny firmly. "Snap out of it. We have to keep going. Kip needs you to get home. What would he do without you? We have to have courage." He paused, then nipped.

"Ouch," said Cress, because Finny had bitten her on the tail.

"I had to do that," said Finny. "You were closing down on me. Welcome back to reality. We have to stick together."

"I don't need your opinion," she said sharply. Sounding so much like Mama. But that was a lie. She did need Finny's opinion, and his friendship. She just wasn't ready to say so right now.

"You know," said Finny, "you can be a hard nut to crack."

"Tell me about it," said Cress. "I'm no good for anything. I'm too young to stay home and watch Kip. That's why we had to move after my father disappeared. I can't babysit, I can't weave, I can't make things. Now I've gotten shipwrecked and lost in the jungle with nothing for supper but a silver whistle. I hate myself."

Finny replied, "I'm not going to wait to hear any more if you're going to go, like, all very-bitter-berry on me. I'll find my own way home."

"Don't let me stop you," said Cress. "I'll just lie down with my paws over my eyes and wait for the Final Drainpipe to come across me."

So Finny bit Cress on the tail again. "Ow, stop that," she said, and bit him back.

He did once more and she ran away from him, and he chased her.

After a while they weren't biting and chasing. They were just running through the wet woods, looking for a way home.

Sometimes not to talk about something, just to do it, is the better idea.

And exercise never hurts. Running made Cress feel strong. Feeling strong made her feel more alive. She felt like avoiding the Final Drainpipe for another evening of life, if she could.

"Look, up ahead," she said. "Is that the moon?"

"It can't be," said Finny, pausing to catch his breath. "The clouds are hiding the moon tonight. But what is it?"

At treetop height, an uncertain light flickered greasily. "We better go closer and see," said Cress.

"No one comes to Two Chimneys without an invitation," said a voice nearby. It was a voice Cress thought she knew. "And no one leaves without permission."

They looked around. They couldn't see a soul in the dark. But then Cress thought she detected a certain note of distinction in the air.

"Is that—could this be Lady Cabbage?" she said aloud.

"The same," said the skunk. "My word! Tiaras and tennis shoes! I'm so glad you've decided to come be my housemaid. And, look, you brought a friend who can be my butler. I love having staff. Welcome to Two Chimneys. Let me show you around."

A shadow detached from under a lilac bush. Going by the smell, it must be Lady Agatha Cabbage, thought Cress. But the skunk had lost her white stripe. She was glossy ebony from head to toe. Perfect camouflage for a dark

night, as it happened. No wonder Cress hadn't been able to see her.

"Oh, yes," said Lady Cabbage, noticing Cress's expression. "I had my fur dyed. What do you think? Does it suit me?"

Cress thought it looked horrible. All she could think to say was, "What about your chinchilla?"

"It got dyed, too," explained the skunk. "To match."

"Howdy," said the chinchilla, a dark shadow of a fur collar. "I've become subtle. Nice to see you again. Now you're caught. She's a jail-keeper."

"Nonsense. I'm a perfectly nice lady of the district," said the skunk. "Please do come in and I'll show you around my country home. It's the most elegant place for miles around. You'll never want to leave."

"You'll never be able to leave," murmured the chinchilla.

"What was I just saying to you?" said Cress to Finny. "The world wants to be difficult. That's what it prefers. That's what it tends to do."

"I'm not the world," said Lady Cabbage. "I'm just little me. Come along."

18

Two Chimneys

The skunk fluffed up her chinchilla collar and scurried through damp undergrowth. Cress and Finian followed. They passed through a ragged kitchen garden. Spring onions and herbs, yum. "The place is going to wrack and ruin," murmured Lady Cabbage. "I must engage a gardener. But good help is so hard to find. And I only have four paws."

"Eight, if you count mine," said the chinchilla. "Free me from my job as a collar, and I'd deadhead the parsley."

"You're ornamental, so be quiet. Clothes aren't supposed to have opinions," said the skunk. "Ah, here we are. Two Chimneys. A lady's home is her castle."

They emerged from stands of weeds into a clearing. Ahead stood a structure of blackened bricks. It rose as tall as trees, and its double chimneys loomed higher, one on either end of the roof.

"Isn't it stunning?" said Lady Cabbage. "It's small, but pretentious."

Three stone steps led to a central front door. Vines curtained some of the lower windows. The upper windows were cracked. A candle guttered in an attic window at the very top. That was the caramel light that Cress had mistaken for the moon.

"Wow," said Cress. She could think of other things to say, but she didn't dare to give offense. There was something a little turnipy about Lady Cabbage.

Mama had been dubious about Lady Cabbage. And the super had said to avoid Two Chimneys. But here they were. "We'll use the servants' entrance," said Lady Cabbage, "since you're commoners. Come along."

She trudged around the corner of the structure.

"Is it just me, or is this whole setup sort of spooky?" Finny whispered to Cress.

"Welcome to my humble abode, which isn't really humble. That's just a saying," said Lady Cabbage. "The humble part."

When they had cleared the front of the building, they

saw that a good deal of the place had fallen in upon itself. A staircase clung to a side wall, giving access to broken ledges and beams. More like shelves than rooms. But a skunk doesn't need a lot of floor space.

Lady Cabbage pranced up a board that slanted against a charred newel post. She crossed to the banister beside the steps. Cress and Finny followed her all the way to the top of the house.

Though open to the elements, the place smelled foul.

"It's not me," said Lady Cabbage. "It's the smell of smoke and soot. This was a human house before I inherited it. It burned down. Apparently two chimneys weren't enough to contain the blaze."

"A human house?" Cress hadn't come upon the concept before. "What do you mean, human?"

"People," said the skunk. "You know. Human critters. Walk on two legs, talk all the time as if they know everything? Very boring folks. And dangerous. But don't worry. They're gone and won't come back. They can't live in a building without proper floors or a standing roof."

"These steps are steep. Are humans tall, like Tunk the Honeybear?" asked Cress.

"Onions and oysters, enough about humans. They depress me," said the skunk. "Now, little bunny cottontail, let's discuss your chores as my live-in parlor maid."

"I'm sorry," said Cress. "I didn't come here to be your maid."

Lady Cabbage looked confused. "Oh. I thought your mother had sent you here because she got tired of you."

"No," said Cress. "She might be tired of me, but she would never send me away to you."

"I don't like the way you say that," replied the skunk, "but never mind. Now that you're here, you will be my maid. I insist. You can do the dusting and make my breakfast. I'll keep you in clover if you pick it yourself, little floppy-ears."

"She has a name," said Finny bravely. "Cress. And so do I. Mine is Finian Oakleaf."

"I don't care if your name is Squirrel Nutface," said the skunk. "I'll get to you later. Now, as you can see, little missy, this place needs tarting up. I spend most of my days attending to the care of my hair, so I can't go around dusting and decorating. I'll rely on you for that. Two Chimneys has great bones, but it has fallen on hard times."

"So have I," said Cress.

The skunk wasn't listening to her. "My little heap of heaven needs to be brought back to its former elegance. Also you can tell me stories when I'm bored. I have a lazy mind and a weak one, so I can't think up things for myself. I remember you are fanciful, no? A wordsmith?"

"This is all wrong," said Cress. "We have to go home."

"You've only just arrived. Stay awhile," said Lady Cabbage. "Like, forever. As for you, Master Nutterkins, let me show you the wine cellar. You can bring me my sherry of an evening. Rubies and radishes, but I've always wanted a butler! And you can keep each other company. I engaged a single servant recently, but the creature upped and bolted. Too lonely. So a pair of you at once—what an improvement! Come along."

Cress shot Finny a look: We'll make a break for it as soon as her back is turned. Anything in the wild woods is better than this. Finny nodded.

If you wanted to stay alive, it was better to have a friend along, she decided.

Lady Cabbage led the way through her boudoir. The nook was filled with jewelry, pots of dye, and piles of false eyelashes made out of cobwebs stiffened with egg white. "You'll have fun fulfilling my every whim," she told Cress and Finny. "You'll come and go when I ring my little bell."

"I'm her little bell," said the chinchilla. "When she shakes me, I have to call out, 'Ring, ring!' It's no fun. I get a headache. Also I'm tone-deaf."

Back downstairs, where ferns tried to grow through rubble, the skunk led them into a basement hole. Hidden below the hearthstones, it proved to be more or less intact.

Jars of hardened maple syrup on rotting shelves, a rocking horse, a chest or two. Beyond, a door of iron bars opened into a small room made all of brick.

"Here's the wine cellar," she said. "I store midnight snacks in here, away from prowlers. Help yourselves."

Cress and Finny had lost their lunch sacks up at the pond's edge. They'd had nothing to eat since breakfast. They were ravenous. So they followed her inside to look.

Lady Cabbage circled around them, a swirl of darkness like a smelly wind. She flicked herself out the door before they knew it. Slamming the iron door, she locked them in.

"This is a wine cellar," she said through the bars. "So you can stay here and whine, whine, whine all you want. As you would say, little squirrel-socks: Joke."

In the dark, as the skunk waddled away, Cress and Finny could hear the chinchilla saying, "I don't think that was very funny."

"Nobody asked for your opinion," replied the skunk. "Clothes aren't allowed to have a sense of humor, anyway."

"How can they be your servants if you keep them locked up?" asked the chinchilla.

"You've heard of a little thing called chains?" said Lady Cabbage, all singsongy.

After a pause, the chinchilla observed, "You really are a skunk."

"So I've been told," replied Lady Cabbage. "But the last domestic ran away the moment my back was turned. That rabbit was trouble. I'm not taking any chances this time."

19

UNDER LOCK AND KEY

The prison, the dark, the being lost. It all fell behind the bright glow of hope. "What if that rabbit she was talking about was my papa?" said Cress to Finny. "Maybe he's just escaped and is looking for us!"

Finny said carefully, "I don't want to stomp on your hopes, but it's hard to see a grown-up male rabbit being confused for a parlor maid, even by a loony old skunk."

"You're stomping," Cress replied crossly. She lolloped back and forth, fuming and hoping.

They had to get out. They tried to chew their way out, but the iron bars made their teeth ache. The floor was a single piece of slate they couldn't dig through. The bricks stayed put.

And no snacks were hidden in the dark corners of the cell. There wasn't even any wine except an empty bottle holding the ghost of elderberry cordial. The place smelled a little like a bathroom.

Finally they flopped upon the floor, worn out. "Do you think your brothers are looking for us?" asked Cress.

"Of course," said Finny. "And my parents. They wouldn't let us just sail off into the sunset like that. What about your mother?"

"She has to take care of Kip," said Cress. "It's all about Kip. Her sick baby." She told Finny how she had tracked her mother to the hemlock tree where she was scoring some honey for Kip, and about meeting Tunk at midnight. Telling the story helped the time pass. For about one minute.

"Your mother must have been so proud of you," said Finny.

"Are you kidding?" asked Cress. "Mama grounded me for going out at night without permission. Now, first time I'm allowed out, I get both shipwrecked and kidnapped. I can't catch a break."

When it grew too cold, Finny and Cress sat with their spines against each other for warmth. Cress had the better deal, she thought, because Finny's big tail made a natural pillow for her to lean into.

"What do you want to do when you grow up?" asked Finny, to pass the time.

Cress said, "I don't think about growing up anymore. I can't imagine it. I can't imagine getting there."

"I'm going to be an aerial gymnast," said Finny. "What with my natural balance, you know. It would allow me to join the circus and travel. I don't want to stay home forever."

"Well, that's very interesting. But not to me," said Cress.

"Are you about to get cranky again?" asked Finny.

"Excuse me?" asked Cress. "We've been jailed by a skunk. I have a perfect right to be cranky."

"Well," said Finny, "you be cranky and I'll be useful. What do we have that we can bargain with? I mean, like, to buy our freedom?"

"We have your fat cushy tail that Lady Cabbage can use for another fur collar," said Cress.

"Rudeness is one thing, but that's just cruel," said Finny. He moved to the other side of the cell, into the darker dark.

"Oh, okay," said Cress, trying not to go statue-still again. "Don't forget. We still have that whistle."

"I have the whistle," Finny reminded her. There was a pause. "But you've made a good point. If I blow on it, what will happen?"

"It will disturb her sleep," said Cress. "Might make her angry."

Finny said, "Maybe she'll let us go then. So things can quiet down."

"Well, she also could kill us," said Cress. "Then we'd be quiet. Joke."

Finny asked, "What could we offer her in exchange for our freedom?"

"How about the whistle?" asked Cress.

"If she wanted this, she could just grab it through the bars," said Finny.

Cress said, "Whether it was my father or not, there was another rabbit here not long ago. Lady Cabbage really wants a maid. Could we nominate anyone else for the job?"

Finny was appalled. "We can't trick anyone into taking our places. Lady Cabbage isn't an ideal boss, locking up her staff like this. No, we have to think of something we can offer to go and get for her."

"She's pretty vain." Cress pictured the skunk's boudoir. "Maybe a mirror?"

Finny thought this a good idea, but he didn't know where they might find a mirror. So that was out. "Could you offer to write her a real-life story about herself?" asked Finny.

"And call it 'A Slice of Lady Cabbage'?" asked Cress, snorting. "I don't think so. Anyway, I can't write stories. I can't make anything up."

Then Cress got an idea. "But, Finny, my mother makes things. Maybe we could offer Lady Cabbage fabric art! She could hang some on her scorched walls. Remember how she said she needed help bringing Two Chimneys back to its old glory? Tapestries would help."

"Sounds like a plan," said Finny. "I'll raise the alarm. Even if Tunk hears it, or the Final Drainpipe, it's worth a try. This is an emergency."

Finny began to blow on the whistle. Short, urgent bursts in groups of three. Somewhere in the woods, voles and beavers might be having bad dreams. But the prisoners heard a scratchy scurrying upstairs. Down into the basement hustled Lady Cabbage, carrying a candle and a small purse. She wore a chinchilla-trimmed nightie.

"Mercy and marzipan! A skunk needs her beauty sleep, you know," she snapped. "What is all this racket?"

Finny and Cress proposed the deal. If Lady Cabbage let them go, they would run home and tell Cress's mother. They were sure she would be willing to weave tapestries for Lady Cabbage.

"It's a good idea, but can I trust you to drag your mother back here?" asked Lady Cabbage.

"Look who's talking about trust," said Cress. "You promise us a snack and you lock us up instead."

"A minor error. Sorry about that," said the skunk. "I'll find you something soon. Tell me about your mother's work."

"It's beautiful," said Cress. "She's got great color sense. She's doing late summer pears against pink leaves at the moment. It'll be the new look of the season. You'll be the first to have it."

"Sounds divine," said Lady Cabbage. "I dance on the cutting edge of fashion. But what if she doesn't do what you ask her?"

"I'll do what I think best," said Mama. Oh, Mama! Standing at the top of the basement steps, trembling like

a walking volcano wrapped in rabbit fur and about to blow its top. "Lady Cabbage, you open that lock at once before I choke you with your own chinchilla."

"Don't do that," said the chinchilla.

20

FRICASSEE

Company, at this hour?" said Lady Cabbage, and she began to apply some makeup.

Mama said again, "Didn't you hear me? I said: Open the door."

"Why?" Lady Cabbage puckered her lips and smacked them, to line up the lipstick, while Mama came closer.

"Because I said so." Mama's say-so was only standard mother-talk, but it seemed to work with Lady Cabbage.

The skunk dug out a key from her beaded purse. "But before I do—"

"Open the door first," said Mama, a steel flute on a single note, "and we can talk after."

Mama clearly meant business. The skunk swung wide the iron gate. Cress and Finny darted out and into Mama's arms. Her hug was generous enough for both of them at once.

"Caviar and castanets, I didn't mean any harm," said Lady Cabbage. "I locked them in for their own protection. Didn't want them wandering off and getting lost at night. Like my last maid."

Cress couldn't contain herself. "Was your last maid my father?"

"A male maid?" Lady Cabbage clutched her chinchilla more tightly about her neck as if for modesty. "Hush your mouth. I keep a wholesome home. Gentlemen for maids! The idea! In fact, my last maid was some snippety saucy young rabbit of no standing at all."

Cress felt her shoulders sag—she had wanted reunion hugs from both parents. Keeping Cress clenched at her side, Mama bristled on. "I don't talk to skunks like you," said Mama. "Get out of my way. We're going home."

"You must understand," said Lady Cabbage. "I require staff to keep me company. A chinchilla is stylish but it doesn't have an interesting point of view. So I get lonely. No one wants to live with a skunk."

"I guess not, if you treat guests like this," said Mama. "This place is a nightmare."

"See what I mean?" The skunk wrung her paws. "I do my best, but I just can't keep up."

"That's no excuse for kidnapping," said Mama. "You deserve prison."

"I didn't mean to hurt anyone's feelings. I only borrowed these two youngsters," said Lady Cabbage. She lay down in the sooty damp. "Oh, okay. Just lock me in my own jail and let me die. Go ahead. Slam the door. I deserve it."

"You still have the key," Mama pointed out. "You put it back in your purse. You'd just unlock the door."

The skunk shrugged. "Well, I might recover my will to live. Especially if you bring me some new wall hangings to jazz things up."

"I don't owe you a thing," said Mama. "You owe us an apology."

"*Sor-ry,*" said the skunk in a voice that failed the sincerity test.

"When my new work is off the loom," said Mama, "come for a private viewing. I'll sell to anyone. I have mouths to feed. But you'd need a lot of it. Frankly, this place is too big for one animal living all alone."

"One and a half," suggested the chinchilla. "Counting me as the half, because I'm small."

"And," said Mama, "it's too close to the humans."

"Oh, Mama," said Cress, finding her voice at last. "Do you know about humans, too? Why didn't you ever tell me?"

"Sweetie-cakes," said Mama, "there's a reason they call it Hunter's Wood. It has to do with hunters. I mean those humans. They can be nasty pieces of work. Snakes and bears and hawks are bad enough, but humans are the hunters we have to worry about most."

"Okay, I'm worried," said Finian. "I'm there. I mean, I'm right there. Got it. Real worried. I just developed a worry wart on my forehead. Let's go home."

"Don't leave me," said Lady Cabbage.

They didn't reply. They climbed the steps out of the basement and walked away as Lady Cabbage cried softly into her chinchilla.

At the bottom of the kitchen garden, they glanced back. From here, the house still looked like a pile of menace, with its dark façade and those two ruined chimneys. But you could tell it was empty behind its severe front—a skeleton, a shambles. A false hull of a home.

They turned to the woods. "How did you find us?" Cress asked her mother.

Mama said, "Finny's brothers told their parents. Lolly Oakleaf fainted on the riverbank when she heard. Dr. Oakleaf had to tend to her. So the boys scurried back to the

Broken Arms to let me know. Manny insisted on baby-sitting Kip so I could set out to look for you."

"All alone?" asked Cress.

"I had help," said Mama. She gestured overhead. "Romeo and Harriet."

"Who?"

"The songbirds," explained Mama. "They flew above me, looking for clues. We followed the stream. By night-fall we'd discovered the broken slats of your raft, washed ashore. I didn't know where you might have gone from there. But the songbirds heard the emergency whistle blowing from the grounds of Two Chimneys. So I found my way, and found you. That's what mothers do."

Cress couldn't quite say thank you, but Finny could, and did. The birds led them home, tweeting signals of direction from the limbs ahead of them.

The dark woods. Will it always be a dark woods, this life? wondered Cress. Filled with eerie, dangerous quiet?

But it got noisier when the songbirds led them to a sloping path to the tableland. A ruckus! Papa? breathed Cress. No. A pale, spotted yellowish creature was fussing in the midst of a brambly hedge.

"Stuck!" said the bundle, a flailing storm of feathers. "And no one to help a lost critter like me!"

"What seems to be the matter?" said Mama, drawing closer.

The creature fixed Mama with a beady eye. "Oh, you're not the farmer. Blessings abounding? Could you unwind this creeper from my foot? I've blundered into trouble, and no mistake. It's my special talent? Blunder? Blunder night and day."

The poor figure stood still as Mama tried to help. "I can see you're not a hen born and raised in Hunter's Wood," said Mama evenly. "Hold still and count to ten."

Mama's calm helped the captive keep still. When the captive was freed, she blundered back and forth, flexing her limbs and wings, clucking up a storm.

"You want to keep your voice down," said Mama. "There is a certain Monsieur Reynard abroad who often enjoys chicken for dinner."

"I take your point," said the hen, and stood as still as a hen statue.

"Where are you going?" asked Mama.

"Away from the fox? Away from the farm?" replied the hen. "Anywhere free of blunder and death."

Mama told the hen to come along with them, at least for a while. Safety in numbers. The hen told them she didn't have a name, really, but last week whenever the farmer saw her, he shook his head and kept saying, "Fricassee, Sunday." That was when the hen decided to emigrate.

So Mama called her Fricassee Sunday. The hen strutted along with them. She was a dizzy creature, even for a hen. Half the things she said sounded like questions, and maybe they were, or maybe it was a regional accent.

There goes Mama, thought Cress, saving each creature in her path. It must be tiring.

When they got to the Broken Arms, everyone was still up, hoping for news. Tears were shed. Manny's wife hobbled out onto their little porch and tossed down some golden dandelion blossoms like confetti.

Lolly Oakleaf hugged Finny so hard, it looked as if she were trying to tuck him into her armpit for safekeeping. Dr. Oakleaf said, "Ahem, ahem," a lot, as if he were going to make a speech, but he never did.

The songbirds tweeted about it. Romeo and Harriet—
that was who they were. Now Cress knew their names.

Even Mr. Owl called down, "As I'm nocturnal, I don't
mind all this hullabaloo at midnight. But we don't want to
draw attention to ourselves in case the Final Drainpipe is
about. Make a note of it."

"Oh, hang the Final Drainpipe!" cried Dr. Oakleaf, finding his voice at last. "The lost have been found, the dead
have come back to life! Somebody pop a cork! Draw a pint
of beer! Somebody play a hornpipe!"

The songbirds launched into a rowdy hootenanny,
and most of the animals stepped lively to the beat. Even
Fricassee Sunday kicked up her talons and favored the crowd
with a yodeling descant.

Everyone joined in but Cress. She headed inside
to catch a glimpse of Kip and see for herself that he was
safe.

"Hey there, kiddo," whispered Manny, giving her a
thumbs-up. "Told them all to stop their blubbing. Knew
you'd be back. You're a survivor."

When Cress had kissed Kip in his crib, she crept
outside again. She crouched in the shadows to watch the
impromptu festival.

All the dead had not come back to life. All the lost had

not been found. Papa was still gone. Now he felt even more gone. And yet the world was dancing. She was still here. There was music, joking, laughter. What did this mean? How could this be?

21

FREEDOM AND BLUNDER

At dawn, Kip stood up in his crib and gripped the railing and cried, "Uppy, Cwessie!" He liked waking up and finding himself alive in the morning. It made him happy for some reason.

By the time Cress crossed the carpet to get him, Kip had noticed Fricassee Sunday roosting on Mama's loom. "Papa?" said Kip.

"Oh, look, a baby," said Fricassee. "Sometimes a blunder, sometimes not."

"No BABY," said Kip, sitting back down in his crib and sucking Rotty.

"You look like a baby to me," said Fricassee. "A baby MONSTER."

"Rowrrr," said Kip, showing his teeth.

"I'm so scared," said the hen placidly. "Think I'll lay an egg and take the pressure off." She did, right there. An egg rolled onto the carpet.

"How do you do that?" asked Cress. "I wish I could make something like that!"

"It's called talent," said the hen. "Talent, and good breeding. I have some Rhode Island forebears. Look out, here comes another."

Mama loped in, droopy and flustered. She set down a small pot of warm honey.

"Are you kidding me?" asked Cress. "After hunting for us all night, you went out again?"

"We were low on honey, and I wanted to beat Tunk to the supply," said Mama, yawning. "I knew you'd be safe with a guest in the house." She didn't notice the eggs. She fell asleep facedown on the carpet.

"Let's go grab some grubs for breakfast," said Fricassee. "We'll let her catch forty winks."

"Okay," said Cress. "Can you teach me how to lay an egg?"

"No," said the hen. "It's a trade secret. Oops, here comes a third. Excuse me just a moment."

"I wonder if Mr. Owl would like eggs," said Cress. "We're way behind on our rent. Mama is too tired to harvest moths every night. She falls asleep."

"He wants them, he can have them. Works for me," said Fricassee. But Kip, out of his crib, had rushed to the eggs to hold them and love them and sit on them. And then he needed a bath, because the eggs were no longer of this world. Cress nearly said "Yolk!"

So Fricassee and Cress each took Kip by the paw and tiptoed out of the flat, leaving Mama in snores on the floor.

"Wait," called Mr. Owl, that busybody from on high. "You'd better leave your mama a note about where you're going. She's been through enough as it is."

"There's no privacy in this place," whispered Cress to Fricassee.

"I heard that," said Mr. Owl. "Make a note of it. In fact,

take one of those small hinged pages that Dr. Oakleaf gave you and write your mother. Make a note of it. Joke!"

"Everyone is saying that now," said Cress. "It's so tired." Still, she took the landlord's advice. She went inside and wrote: We're going out.

On the other side of the paper, she drew a musical note. She stuck it on the loom where her mother would see it.

Back outside, she called to Mr. Owl, "I made a note of it."

"That's the ticket," he replied.

The Broken Arms was low-key this morning. The Oakleaf family was sleeping off the party of the night before. The songbirds hadn't sung matins; they were still resting their heads under their wings. Manny and Sophie Crabgrass sat on their fire escape, warming their fur in the sunshine. Sophie groomed her tail, and Manny was reciting baseball scores to her in a low voice. They waved but didn't holler.

Fricassee Sunday settled under the willow tree and worried nits out of her pinfeathers. In the shallows where the willow leaves dragged in the water, Cress splashed Kip clean of eggy mess.

"It's peaceful here," said Fricassee. "No blunder to speak of? I hardly know what to do with myself." A couple of beavers were heading downstream, probably intending to build a new dam, cause a flood, create havoc of some sort. Blunder always seemed to be in the schedule, sooner or later. But not right now. "What do you call this neighborhood?" asked the hen.

"The apartment tree is called the Broken Arms. The rest is . . ." Cress looked around at the place, and all the creatures going about their business without complaint. "I suppose it's just hereabouts," she said. "I don't know if it has another name."

"Your mother called it Hunter's Wood?"

"Oh, that's the name for the whole world, I think," said Cress. "This is just a small part of it. It's just here. It's not home."

"Why not?" asked Fricassee.

Cress told the hen about the disappearance of Papa. She told how the Watercress family had had to move out of their warren. "It was nicer there," said Cress. "It felt like home. It was bigger and more private. We had three rooms and a pantry and a back door. And our own carrot garden. And I had rabbit friends."

"Well, you have lots of friends here, as I saw last night," said Fricassee. "But I have no one? I left my all my sisters behind? No one on that farm has a spirit of adventure, I'll tell you that! Or maybe I got locked out of the chicken yard because I was keeping an eye on some seed corn behind the gate. It's all a blunder. I can't remember? Anyway, I can't go back there. What am I to do?"

Cress was too polite to say "You can't live with us," but that's what she was thinking. The single room was tight as it was, and Kip was going to keep growing. And so, she supposed, was she.

"Home is a funny idea," said Fricassee Sunday. "It's mostly a safe place, but sometimes they plan to kill you and eat you. Out here is wild, but you can still get eaten? I don't know which is better? But I know I don't want to go back there."

"Why not?" asked Cress.

"I think," said Fricassee, "it's something called freedom? Which is thrilling but worrying? Because it's such a blunder?"

Cress remembered being locked in the wine cellar, and she had to agree. Freedom was thrilling, and it was worth it, even when the world held in its paws the likes of Monsieur Reynard and the Final Drainpipe, not to mention Tunk the Honeybear, eagles, hawks, humans, pollen, blunder, Lady Cabbage, floods, and carrot root rot.

"I wish there were other rabbits around," said Cress.

"I wish I were a rabbit, then," said Fricassee Sunday.

"You make a better hen," said Cress, feeling she'd been rude.

"No one has ever said that to me before," said Fricassee. "Some have said I'd make a better stew, but that's about it for the compliments."

Kip got tired of the stream. He came up the bank, soaking wet and a little shivery. He wanted to sit in Fricassee Sunday's lap, but the hen didn't have a lap. So he huddled in Cress's arms and sang to Rotty.

The hen sighed. Cress sighed, too. All the weight of the world, and all its luxury, seemed to be holding its breath in this bell-shaped space marked by the dragging branches of a waterside willow tree. It felt like a grown-up moment, both risky and splendid. Cress wished her mother were there to say the right thing. Or her father.

Just this moment she could hardly remember what her father's voice sounded like.

Still, Cress managed to offer this: "Fricassee, today might not be good. But it might be good enough."

"That sounds like something in a book," replied the hen. "Not that I ever read one."

22

TEMPER, TEMPER

The next day Kip came down with a bad cough. "Spring flu," said Mama.

"Is it because I bathed him in the stream?" asked Cress.

"Stop thinking you're responsible for the world," said Mama. "Flu is flu, end of story. Make a note of it."

If Cress didn't have to be responsible, maybe she didn't have to be good. She was tired of being good. Being good was a blunder. When Kip cried for his Rotty and Mama discovered the stuffed carrot hidden in a curve of the carpet, Mama knew it was Cress's fault. She sent Cress outside.

"What if Monsieur Reynard comes along to eat me?" shouted Cress. "You'll be sorry."

Mama didn't answer. But she slammed the door. Mama in a temper, too? Not often, and no fun.

Cress stood on the doorsill wondering how to annoy her mother some more. But just then Manny came strolling along in a white boater and a seersucker vest, twirling his cane and looking dapper as April.

"Your mama at home, kiddo?" he asked.

"Where else you think she would be?" asked Cress.

"Oooh, someone ate thorns for breakfast," said the mouse.

"I don't mean to be rude," said Cress. "Not to you, anyway. But nothing is going right."

"I know what you mean," called Mr. Owl from his perch. He cleared his throat. "The seashore sounds delightful at this time of year, but who can get away?"

The old mouse snapped a salute to his boss. To Cress he said, "I have to stop by your place and give your mother a talking-to."

The door flew open. Mrs. Watercress must have been standing inside, listening. She had her baby in her arms, and her kerchief was askew. "What is it now, Manny? This isn't a good time. Kip has a fever."

"The landlord says you're three days behind with the rent," said Manny. "Also he has to charge you more. The rent is going up."

"Going up? For this moldy hole?" asked Mama. Oooh, this so wasn't one of her good days.

"He's noticed you've taken in a lodger," continued the super. "That blunderbuss hen. So he has to charge you more rent. The flat is only zoned for three."

"The flat should be zoned for a single pancake," said Mama. "We can hardly breathe in here. And Fricassee Sunday isn't living with us. She's only visiting. We're allowed to have guests, aren't we?"

"Actually, no," called Mr. Owl. "Sorry. Those are the rules. You owe me back rent of thirty dead moths plus three extra for the hen."

"Are you heartless?" asked Mama in a rising tone. "And me with a sick child? We're out of ginger root for his tea, and his sister is a constant worry, and I'm trying to get my fall line into production. I'm busy past midnight. I can't work miracles."

"I'll come by a little later," said Manny. "To help you pack, I mean. I'm not sure this place is working out for you lot."

"You show up back here and I'll hit you over the head with your own cane," said Mama. This time she slammed the door so hard that the latch broke off.

Cress was ashamed of her mother and still out of sorts with her. But she couldn't stand by silently. "Raising the rent? You have some nerve," Cress called up to Mr. Owl. "Make a note of it!"

"Kid, enough is enough," whispered Manny.

"Little one," called Mr. Owl to Cress, "grow up. A deal's a deal." He ruffled his feathers and rotated his head halfway around on his neck, as if ready to look at something else.

"Don't you turn your back on me!" she shouted. Papa had always said that when he was angry: Don't you turn your back on me! "I mean, the back of your head."

"Everybody's spiking a spring fever today, boss," called Manfred Crabgrass. "Pay her no mind. She's upset about her brother."

"Sending this old mouse to make trouble for us!" shouted Cress to the owl. "Why don't you come down here and sort this out for yourself?"

Manny's wife, Sophie Crabgrass, appeared at her window. Behind the glass, Sophie shook her head, an urgent message of NO for Cress.

But Cress had gone over the edge and she couldn't stop herself. "My father is DEAD and my brother is SICK and my mother is working herself to the BONE and you have the GALL to send some twerpy MOUSE to try to wring BLOOD out of a STONE?"

All at once Cress was on the ground. She thought blind Mr. Owl had swooped down at last, zeroing in on her through the noise of her fury. He would sweep her up in his talons and eat her as rent. But she wasn't airborne, only suffocating. She was under a heap of squirrels doing an intervention. They had jumped from two flights up.

"Got this covered, boss," called Manny. "Covered by the Oakleaf family. All six of them. I'll bring you the Watercress family's back rent soon as I get it. Have a nice day."

Cress couldn't see what Mr. Owl was doing, if anything, because the world was cloaked in squirrel fur. But at least the landlord wasn't answering. "Cress," whispered

Finian, "you're a bit of a nut job today. Did you know that?"

"I hate you most. Did you know that?" replied Cress. Which was a lie, but it was the first thing out of her mouth. Out of loyalty, one of Finny's brothers bit her on the tail. She couldn't tell which brother.

"Okay, you've subdued the rogue element. Now bundle her out of here," called Manny. So the Oakleaf family escorted Cress down the path away from the Broken Arms.

"Get your paws off me," said Cress. "I can walk by myself."

Fricassee Sunday was flumping along behind, breathing in rapid bursts. "It's all my fault, isn't it? I'm such a blunder. I'll leave? I'll pack my bags as soon as I can buy some? I'll need a suitcase with little wheels? Sometimes I keep some of my eggs as souvenirs. It's all the family I have, until they crack under the strain. Probably of having me as their mother."

"Fricassee," shouted Cress, and almost continued, "Shut up." But that would be a rudeness too far. This rent disaster wasn't the hen's fault. It was Mr. Owl's. Even during moments of anger, fairness sometimes comes to call. Cress swallowed her comment down.

"Yes?" Fricassee bobbed her head around to look at the rabbit girl.

"You and I need to go hunting for some ginger root," Cress said. To the Oakleaf family, she added, "I've got myself under control. Goodbye."

"I'll come, too," said Finny.

Cress glanced at him with disbelief. She wasn't ready for her bad mood to be that improved. But there he was.

"What, you never heard of something called loyalty?" he said. "After all we've been through?"

"Watch out for the Final Drainpipe, kiddos," called Manny as they headed across the stream and up the hill on the other side.

Beyond the hill and the stream, some lilacs had just bloomed. They smelled sweetly ordinary, and better than usual. Just what Cress wasn't expecting. How the world likes to be contrary!

23

NASTY

Cress grumbled and sniffed till her bad mood was nearly over.

"You know," said Fricassee Sunday as they scaled the slope on the other side of the stream, "I, too, used to be hot-tempered. Could I get testy? I'll answer my own question. Yes, I could get testy."

"Do I have to hear about this?" said Cress. But she was relieved that her voice came out in a normal way, not all shaky.

"What did you do about your temper?" Finny asked the hen.

"I taught myself to lay eggs? I always say," added Fricassee, "there's nothing like self-expression to help you get over yourself."

Cress hmmmphed. She was sure she couldn't learn how to lay eggs. But there was something in what the hen had said. Cress knew that weaving patterns out of nothing but raw time and random ideas—and wool—seemed to settle Mama somehow. It was how she got through.

"I get your point," said Cress. "But I'm not cut out for self-expression. To do that you need—whatever. I don't know. Something I don't have."

"You need life," replied the hen. "You got that, chickadee. Buckets of it."

The three of them walked apart under the larches on the hillside. Some of the flowers of the trees had fallen in the grass. To climb the hill felt like walking up a tilting floral carpet.

When the terrain became rockier, Cress remembered about the Final Drainpipe, so she veered closer to Finny and Fricassee. But not too close. It felt good to be sort of alone and yet not alone.

Just like being in a family, actually.

They came to a grove in the forest where the ground stank. Cress recognized the tang of last year's gingko berries. She knew. She had gone digging for ginger root with her father once or twice. "We've hit the jackpot," she told the others. "We'll dig up fresh roots. Who knows? Maybe Mr. Owl would accept some as back rent."

"I'm pretty sure owls eat chicken eggs," said Fricassee. "So I am still willing to produce eggs for him. I mean, under contract? Everything on the up-and-up? I'm a hen with a reputation to think about."

"What kind of reputation is that?" asked Finny politely.

"Blunder here, blunder there, little blunders everywhere. Still, I'm known as a solid worker?" The hen preened. "I'm good at stepping up production to meet demand."

They set to their task. Fricassee kept a lookout for the snake or other threats. Rabbits and squirrels are good diggers, so before long Cress and Finny had a trove of ginger root. Too much to bring home at one go. "What we can't carry we'll leave here," Cress told them. "Finny and I can come back tomorrow and get the rest."

Fricassee Sunday led the way back along the ridge. Finny and Cress could barely see over their heaps of ginger root. They didn't know what the hen meant when she said, "Don't move. Strange creature of the wild is staring at us."

It's the Final Drainpipe at last, thought Cress. She dropped all her supplies, and Finny did, too.

"I said don't move?" said Fricassee. "You moved."

"What is it?" asked Cress.

They inched forward. A red-and-white checkered cloth lay upon the ground like a fallen flag. Upon it were set a wicker basket, some fruit and sandwiches, and a bottle of pink fizzy wine, uncorked. A single unblinking creature sat among the lunch. Her legs stretched out at right angles to each other. Ungainly and mannered. Her skin was the color of a cream biscuit, her eyes a fierce unnatural blue. She sported a ridiculous frilled dress and a bonnet with a bow.

"I think she's dead?" whispered Fricassee.

"She might just be blind, like Mr. Owl," said Finny. "She can't see us. Look, she's not turning her head when I frisk my tail about."

"What is she?" asked Cress, who had never seen the like.

"She's a human," said Fricassee Sunday. Her feathers ruffled. "But if she's dead, it's okay for us to take her basket? It'll make it easier to carry the ginger root back."

"Are you demented?" asked a voice. They thought the human child had spoken to them. But her mouth hadn't moved, so they were confounded. Then a second creature poked a nose, some whiskers, and a bright pair of eyes from behind the glassy-eyed human. "Hey, this here's a doll. A doll for humans. A toy."

A young brown rabbit. The first rabbit not related to Cress that she had seen in, oh, weeks and weeks, or more. About her own age.

"How come you have a toy for humans?" asked Fricassee Sunday.

"I'm hanging out, minding my own business," said the rabbit, "when this human family lumbers along and sits down to eat. Then something stirs in the grass. I can hear it slither. They run away, all screamy. So I'm, like, itching to nab some of these eats before the human beanpoles come back."

"The Final Drainpipe!" said Finny. "He loves warm days, and suns himself on the rocks. That's what they say."

"Whaddya know, a snake expert. You're right: there are some warm rocks beyond us," said the rabbit. "Smart for a squirrel-brain. But humans scare snakes as much as snakes scare them. The Final Drainpipe, or whatever it was, it scrammed."

"What an odd toy," said Cress, finding her voice at last. "It looks kind of sick."

"You'd look kind of sick, too, if you were made of plastic hair and wax lips," said the other rabbit. "What hole did you crawl out of, anyway? I don't think I know you."

"I live in a place called the Broken Arms," said Cress. "Fricassee and Finian here are—"

For some reason it was hard to name them as her friends. Not to another rabbit, and a girl rabbit at that. "They are my hunting party," she finished. "This is Hunter's Wood. We were hunting ginger root."

Finny noticed Cress's caution. He made a face. "Really, Cress?" he said. "Hunting party? Are you sure I'm not your butler?"

"We'll take that basket," said Fricassee, deciding to be the grown-up, more or less. "As long as no one seems to want it? Thank you very much and goodbye? Forever."

"Nice to meet you, too," said the rabbit. She rolled her eyes at Finny; he must have been too perky for her. To Cress she said, "Nasty."

"That's not polite? In my book?" said the hen. "Anyone who calls someone they just met nasty must be, well, sort of nasty herself."

"I am." The rabbit sat on her haunches and looked in

the other direction as if bored. She put on a pair of sunglasses. They must have belonged to the doll because they were big on the rabbit's face. Cress adored them and wanted a pair just like them. "I am Nasty," said the other rabbit. "That's my name. Natasha Nasturtium, but everyone calls me Nasty. I'm a piece of work, and proud of it."

"I'm Cress," said Cress. "Cress Watercress."

"Want to hang out sometime, Cress? Meet you back here, maybe tomorrow," said Nasty. "Lose your goody-goody pals and get ready to party. But since the human beanpoles might be coming back to get their stuff soon, right now I'm outta here."

She twitched and said to Finian and Fricassee in a stuffy accent, "Frightfully dull to have to dash like this, old chaps. But ta-ta and all that rot." She yawned at them, right in their faces. She looked droll, but hard. And then she was gone, arcing over the ridge.

Fricassee started back down the hill with her little chinless chin high in the air. Finny and Cress grabbed the basket and piled it with ginger root. It was so big and heavy that they had to carry it between them. But they couldn't look at each other. Finny was livid. Cress was in love.

24

OUT ALONE

Mama was glad to see the ginger root. "Cress, this almost makes up for your rudeness to our landlord," she said. "What were you thinking, talking to him like that? You weren't thinking." She began to chop up a small finger of ginger. She put it to steep in a clay pot full of hot water and dropped in a dollop of honey. "Thank you for helping out, Finny," she added. "You are a love."

Finny took off without saying goodbye or you're welcome.

Sprawled on his stuffed carrot, Kip was cranky. His breath, oh, so wheezy. "Woofs on waws!" he cried. "Woofs on waws."

Cress said, "He means he wants the super to come and make wolves on the walls again."

"I think he's seeing things, what with this fever," said Mama. "In any case, I don't care to cross paths with that interfering mouse again today if I can help it. Thank you but no, thanks."

Cress lit a candle. She tried to make a shadow wolf on the wall, but it only looked like a lump of bunny paw. "Everybody can make things but me," she said. "Even Kip is making up things in his fever."

"You can make friends," said Mama. "Faster than I can. Look at Finny."

Cress rolled her eyes about Finny and thought about Nasty instead. Her new—well, she wasn't a friend. Yet.

Fricassee Sunday's mind followed the same path. "By the way?" she said to Mama. "We ran into a nasty rabbit girl up yonder. Rude? Maybe a distant cousin of yours?"

"I have distant cousins," said Mama. "Indeed, I do. Thousands. But none of them are nasty and rude."

Cress pouted. "Her name is Nasty, but she's nice."

Fricassee explained about the footloose rabbit, the monstrous doll, the food, the picnic tablecloth. Cress kept shooting the hen filthy looks. She had wanted to keep Nasty to herself for a while. "Maybe I'd better move out," said Fricassee. "I'm getting the message that I'm in the way here?"

"Look," said Mama. "It's true this place is too small for four. And for all I know, Kip has flu germs."

Kip sneezed, and his nose had to be wiped. So did the opposite wall.

"But, Fricassee Sunday," continued Mama. "It's dangerous out there, what with foxes patrolling the neighborhood. Also that honeybear lumbering about. I'd never forgive myself if I came upon a pile of chicken feathers. All that was left of you."

"You could weave them into your new work as a tasteful memorial tapestry," said Fricassee Sunday.

"Bit of advice for you," said Mama. "Anybody named Fricassee should drop the word 'tasteful' from her vocabulary."

"I'm going to offer Mr. Owl tomorrow's eggs as my share of the rent while I was here," said Fricassee stoutly. "It's the least I can do?"

Mama couldn't talk the hen out of it. Fricassee gave Mama a quick peck on the cheek. "See you around? And, Cress? Watch out for that Nasty character. I don't have a good feeling about her?"

"You make eggs, Mama makes scarves and blankets,

Manny makes shadows. I make friends, that's what I make," said Cress. "Make a note of it."

"Kip make MESS," said her brother, and proved it. Fricassee blundered away.

After Kip had been washed and changed, given his tea, and lullabied to sleep again, Mama tried to tidy the place. She picked up the wicker basket that Cress and Finny had brought the ginger root in. "And where did this come from?" she said, admiring the hinged handles.

"We told you," said Cress. "An abandoned human picnic. Sideways from some gingko trees."

"Humans? So near us?" Mama looked worried. "Cress, that's not good. You have to take this back."

"Why?"

"You know why. Because taking it is stealing. And what if those humans come looking for it?"

"They won't," said Cress.

"They will," said Mama. "They must have a human child who adores that doll. They'll come back for it. And they'll look for their basket. In any case, your father and I didn't raise you to be light-fingered. That's not like you. You'll have to return it."

"Now?"

"Yes, now," said Mama crisply. All no-nonsense when

it came to right and wrong. "Find Finny and ask him to go with you."

"Look," said Cress, "are we going to fight every day from now on? Tell me so I can figure out what vitamins to take for it. This is no fun for me."

"You becoming a teenager already?" said Mama. "Cress, don't start. Just do as I say. You know I can't leave Kip alone. Go get Finny. Safety in numbers. Ditch that basket where you found it before it brings us trouble. And I want you to put it right back where you picked it up. Do you hear me, young lady?"

"I'm a blunder," said Cress. "That's all I am to you."

"If you're going to be theatrical," said Mama, "pick another word. Blunder has been overused lately, in case you haven't noticed."

Cress went out and tried to slam the door, but as the latch was still broken, the door just bounced back open.

She wasn't going to ask Finny to go with her. He was being all weird for some reason.

She decided if she was old enough to get yelled at eight times a day, she was old enough to go out on the slope by herself, whether or not anyone else thought so. And if the Final Drainpipe found her and ate her? She'd become the real bunny spirit of the woodland, no joke.

And that would give Mama and Kip some extra room

in that tiny basement apartment. They'd be glad to get rid of her.

All on her own, Cress started down the path to cross the stream. She could hear Manny shouting something from the fire escape. She ignored him. She put the basket over her head as if it were a bonnet. This felt like something Nasty might do.

The new rabbit might still be hanging out around the picnic ground. Maybe she lived thereabouts. Not that Cress cared, much.

She laughed out loud. It didn't have a nice sound, echoing inside the wicker basket. It sounded skunky, and a little off.

Cress felt as if she were becoming someone different. She wondered who. Maybe that is what growing up was all about—not knowing yourself, over and over again. How tiresome. What if you grew up to be someone you actually didn't like?

25

THE FINAL SOMETHING
OR OTHER

Now that she was truly alone, the hillside was different.

The trees were all in the right spots—slender things, ragged with unfurled leaves. And the hill sloped with the same lazy ambition, trying to get to the top but not in any hurry. But it seemed more alert, the whole place. Keyed up. As if something had changed.

She skirted the stand of gingko trees. The picnic table-cloth had been up over that outcropping of rock, yes? She was sure of it. She lolloped along a little less briskly. She couldn't see over the ridge. What if the human beanpoles had come back to finish their lunch?

When she poked her nose up to sniff for danger, she

couldn't detect the picnic supplies. Maybe she'd taken the wrong path.

In front of her stood several dead trees. Their foliage had browned and fallen off. The bony trunks looked like the spines of large fish standing on their tails.

Between two of the trees billowed a plus-size spiderweb. Four feet wide and just as tall, it put Mama's home weavings to shame. One fat and satisfied spider dozed in the corner. It must have already eaten its fill, because it was ignoring the dead moths and horseflies that had blundered into the sticky strings.

As she stared at the huge web, Cress realized she'd seen

it before. She and Mama and Kip had passed it that night they first made their way to the Broken Arms.

So that meant that their old warren couldn't be far. It was probably down the other side of this slope somewhere.

She had an impulse to run to the old home. Her real home.

But she fought against the instinct. Going back would be a mistake. If she never saw that familiar place again, she could still imagine that Papa was there, just as in the olden days. Waiting for his family to come home. She didn't want to give up that picture in her mind.

Besides, she wanted to finish what Mama told her to do and return. She didn't want to get lost or get dead. Not really.

She veered away from the web. After she had replaced the picnic basket, she could make a detour this way and snatch some of the low-hanging moths. Dead moths could serve as an apology to Mama for Cress being out of sorts. It would be easier than talking.

The spider trembled on the edge of the web, as if sizing up Cress as a possible feast.

"Don't even think about it," murmured Cress.

She angled along the ridge. Before long, she spied the red-and-white checkered cloth. So, no one had come back yet. Just the monstrous human toy, staring with frozen eyes at some crisis on her own horizon. If human toys looked anything like their owners, human beanpoles must be hideous. Cress hoped she'd never have to meet one.

She would just drop the basket where she'd found it, as she had promised Mama she would. Then she would scoot on back the way she'd come, stopping at the web.

But as she approached the red-and-white checkered cloth, another feeling came over her. The air pricked like static. The hillside was on high alert.

A snake in the grass! The Final Drainpipe!

Cress squatted on the red-and-white squares and flipped the picnic basket over her head. Its handles were hinged, so the basket clamped down over her and made a wicker shell, a blind. No one could see her. She could see no one.

She could sense the Final Drainpipe near, though. It felt like ice frying in her blood. Another feeling on this strange and terrible day, a feeling she had never wanted to know about.

Every scrape of wind sounded like the snake slithering through the grass, nearer and nearer.

She tried to calm herself by saying, Cress, maybe it's just the human beanpoles come back for their human things.

But that didn't help. Humans might not be any nicer to rabbits than snakes were.

Also, humans would clump with great, thudding steps.

And a human child would probably smell bad. While a snake would pause . . . and flicker his forked tongue between his fangs . . . and put his head down and slide closer. So stealthy you could hardly hear him, just feel him.

She tried to hold her breath, but she could only do that for a while. So she took short panting breaths instead.

Now that she was inside it, the wicker basket didn't only smell like ginger root. It also smelled like baloney sandwiches. For the entire rest of my life, even if it is very short, like two minutes, thought Cress, death will smell like ginger root and baloney sandwiches.

Then it seemed as if the checkered squares were bulging underneath her. The Final Drainpipe was right here. Sliding directly under the tablecloth.

She wanted to scream, but her voice wouldn't come out. And to whom would she be screaming? She had come here all alone.

The snake, if it was a snake and not just her imagination, was now pretending to be the root of a tree. That narrow, curving hummock outlined by red-and-white checks. Holding perfectly still.

Now something pressed against the wicker basket, rocking it a little. Sniffing to see what was under it.

Cress was going to die. She nearly died just thinking

about it. But all of a sudden her muscles told her she'd rather die running than just waiting around for the experience.

With a kick she flipped the basket over. It hit something that huffed at her. A hot, meaty breath. The world streaked by in a white blur, she ran so fast. She could hear a mouth panting behind her, and galloping feet.

Instinct took over. She zigzagged suddenly to one side and then the other. Her pursuer couldn't turn as swiftly, so she caught sight of him. Not the Final Drainpipe, after all, but Monsieur Reynard. A fox with an appetite.

Cress never realized she could run as fast as she did. She was back at the Broken Arms in about seven seconds.

"Well, that was fast," said Mama, turning around from Kip with a damp washcloth in her hand. "Did you put the basket back where you found it?"

Cress couldn't speak because she was panting so hard. She just nodded. Mama said no more but made her daughter two crackers with peanut butter.

Cress crept under Mama's loom the way she used to do when she was young. She closed her eyes. Snakes and foxes and the wicked, wicked world. To still herself, she listened to Kip breathing with that rattle in his chest. It was the most beautiful sound she had ever heard, the sound of brother.

26

THE SECRET OF THE LANDLORD

Cress stayed in. She played with Kip when he finally woke up. He was still dozy and sweaty. She told him a story about a devil fox and how a rabbit girl learned how to fly to escape him. Mama listened to Cress as she worked double time. "That's quite the tale, Cress," she said at one point. "Make a note of it."

Cress found one of the little tabs of paper and drew another musical note upon it. "Very funny," said her mother. "Are you collecting those notes for a song?"

The shooting shuttles, the banging headers, the thump of the batten pressing each thread against its mates, it all made a nice, private sound of industry. The finished cloth bunched up on Mama's loom. Once she had cut down a piece, she still had to fringe the ends and weave in the selvage strings along the sides. Then she had to wash and size the cloth so it would hang evenly.

Kip and Cress filled a basin of sudsy water to help with that part. While they were waiting, they enacted a naval battle with the sippy cups, floating them among the mounds of suds.

"Someone is feeling better," said Mama. Cress wasn't sure which of her children she meant.

At sunset the door opened. "Well, why bother to knock? The latch is broken, so I walk right in," said the super.

"Manfred Crabgrass, I'm in no mood—" Mama began, but the mouse stilled her with a raised hand.

"I'm the superintendent," he reminded her. "I'm here to fix your broken latch. Monsieur Reynard's been spotted hereabouts, and I don't want either of your kids turning into a snack for a fox." The super threw Cress a sidelong look. He had seen her heading out by herself earlier. But he didn't give her away.

"Manny, about that rent," said Mama.

"I haven't told you yet, Mama," interrupted Cress. "I found a giant spiderweb up the hill. On the far side of the stream. Lots of dead moths stuck to it. More than the spider can eat. We could collect some and make a payment on our back rent."

"Better move fast," said Manny. "Mr. Owl is thinking about evicting you and your family."

"Why would he do that?" asked Cress. "We just got here."

"Well, that hen needs a place to stay, too," said Manny. "And Mr. Owl likes eggs, as it happens. So he's thinking about shaking things up a little. I mean, since you find it hard to get your rent in on time. Nothing personal."

"Everything that happens to persons is personal," said Mama, but the fight wasn't in her. She was too tired.

"Why do we even have to pay?" asked Cress. "Why is this even his building?"

"He's the higher-up," said Manny, shrugging. Cress didn't get it, but grown-up life was still mostly a mystery to her.

Manny took out a little penknife to whittle a new piece for the latch. Kip said, "Wooves on waws."

"Look, I like you guys," said Manny. "I don't want you to move. But Mr. Owl lives on the acorns and the moths and the worms his tenants pay for rent. He's not a public charity."

Cress said, "He hears so well—why can't he navigate by sound, the way bats do? He ought to be able to fly around and feed himself."

"Mind your own business," said Manfred Crabgrass. "A deal's a deal, whisker-cheeks." It was a mystery how he could say such harsh things so kindly.

"Manny," asked Cress, "will you take me to harvest moths tonight?"

"Don't even think about it," began her mother.

"Mama," said Cress, "I'm growing up. I have to take some responsibility here. If I go out with a chaperone, I can get to that spiderweb and back without fuss or bother. You have to let me help. Otherwise I'm just part of the problem."

"Mrs. Watercress," said the super, "your daughter has

a point. Make a payment on your back rent, buy yourself a little time. I'll escort Cress to that web. I know the one she's talking about. It isn't far. We'll be back in a jiffy."

Cress and Manny slipped away. For the third time that day, Cress crossed the stream and headed up the hill on the other side.

The night was clear and warm. Bats zipped about. Toads were chorusing in the distance. Some evening flowers were unloading night aroma so heady that for a moment Cress wondered if Lady Cabbage was strutting about the hillside in her chinchilla and her decided airs.

When they were far enough away for some privacy, Manny said, "Mr. Owl tells me he heard Monsieur Reynard chasing you today. That pesky fox nearly caught you. I didn't want to mention it in front of your mother. But you'd better watch out, little whiskers. Your mother couldn't handle another disaster right now."

Cress replied, "Okay, okay. But I want to ask you about Mr. Owl."

"You're changing the subject," said the super. "So what about him?"

"Mr. Owl isn't blind, is he?" asked Cress. "I'm guessing he's not blind."

The mouse puffed out his cheeks. "What makes you guess such a crazy thing?"

Cress said, "How could any blind owl know as much as he does just by listening? How could he know it was Monsieur Reynard and not some other fox? Why does Mr. Owl tell everyone that he's blind?"

Manny pointed ahead. "There's your web. It's a doozy. You ready?"

They dropped the subject of Mr. Owl as they worked to get the moths. Manny found a long stick. He poked the web at the top. As the hefty spider scaled her thready lattice to check out the commotion, Cress flicked off a few moth corpses from the lower half of the web. "Done," said Manny, ditching the stick. "Thank you lots, Madame Ariadne."

On the way down the hill, Cress said, "Manny, before we get back to the Broken Arms, tell me about Mr. Owl."

The old mouse stopped. He stroked his moustache with both paws. At last he said, "The songbirds aren't aware of this, and the squirrels aren't, either. In fact, only my dear Sophie and I are clued in. Need-to-know basis, me being the super and all. So I don't think it is any of your business, little rabbit. But what can I do? There's something bright and curious about you. I like you, and your family, too. Even if I'm going to have to evict you sooner or later. The truth is, sugar-pie, Mr. Owl has never flown a stroke in his life."

Cress's mouth gaped open. She patted her sack as if the

dead moths might be so startled that they would come to life and fly away.

"The Broken Arms?" continued Manny. "Both his wings are broken. He can't fly. Mr. Owl was hatched in that penthouse. He was born that way. He's never left his perch. So you're right, little missy detective. He isn't blind. That's a story he tells to explain why he doesn't come down. He's spent his whole life at the top of the dead tree. That's why he needs tenants to bring him food. Otherwise he'd starve."

"That's so sad. How can life be so sad? I can't believe it," said Cress, but that wasn't true. She could believe it just fine.

"If you say a word about this to anyone," said Manny, "I'll have to break both *your* arms."

He was kidding about the threat, but not about the command. Cress nodded.

They walked in silence down the hill, hopped across the stream, and parted without saying goodbye. Only as she was closing the door with the repaired latch did Cress realize that she hadn't seen the moon sailing in the cloudless sky tonight. The sky was starry, but bereft of its one great night-light.

27

LULLABY FOR A
MOONLESS NIGHT

Kip was asleep in his crib. Mama took the moths from Cress and laid them out on a napkin. There were nine. One had a broken wing. That was all right. It was dead already.

Mama heated up a cup of milk and set it down in front of Cress. Then she sat in her rocking chair and pulled it closer to the table.

"What's the matter?" she asked. "Tell me."

Cress held her teacup. Two tears fell from her eyes and almost salted her milk.

"You went out alone earlier today," said Mama. "Is that it?"

Cress glanced at Mama in surprise but shook her head.

Mama tried again. "Finny came by looking for you after

you had gone," she said. "I was upset that he wasn't with you. You disobeyed me. Is that why you're crying?"

Cress shook her head again. The tears were more fulsome now, and she used her paws to wipe her face.

"Were you scared by something out there? Did you get in trouble? You can tell me anything," said Mama. "You know, sweetie, there's little in this world I haven't heard of. Or already seen for myself. I'm not easily startled by life anymore."

Cress put her head, cheek-down, on the table and looked at her mother. Mama seemed to swim in a pool of tears. Then Mama held out her arms, and Cress left her stool and climbed into her mother's lap.

When she could speak, Cress said, "The moon is gone."

"Shhh. You'll wake up Kip. What do you mean?"

Cress told her mother that the moon, which had been changing its shape every night, had finally melted away. It was gone, as gone as Papa.

"Ah," said Mama. "I see. But, my darling Cress, the moon will grow back. It comes and goes. Just like sorrow. I mean it. Sorrow goes and comes. It waxes and wanes—those are words for how the moon grows and gets full and then diminishes, melts away. Over and over. It always comes back. It's part of life. You get used to it. You learn you can live through the moonless nights."

Cress cried harder.

"I know," said Mama, rocking and petting. Mothers know everything. "I know. The moon will go away and come back, but Papa won't. I know. And your memories of him will seem to fade. But then they'll come back. I promise. Your love of him sometimes will be eclipsed by other things. Like fear. And, yes, by other joys. Really. And your love of him will come back. He won't come back, our dear Papa.

But he hasn't left us for good as long as we cherish him and remember him."

Cress had to wipe her nose. She climbed down and grabbed the first cloth she could find. All the moths went on the floor. "Never mind about that," said Mama. Cress climbed back in her lap and closed her eyes.

"Kip won't remember, will he," said Cress. Not a question.

"Would you please be quiet and let me sing you a lullaby?" asked Mama. "I haven't sung to you in a long time."

She sang a pretty song, about daisies in May, and a silly song about frogs at a wedding, and then a sleepy song, a lullay-lullay song. She didn't have a very good voice. It didn't matter.

28

FEVER

In the morning Kip's fever was spiking again. Mama asked Cress to call Dr. Oakleaf. So Cress went outside and hollered yoo-hoo.

"You're making an unholy hullabaloo," called Mr. Owl from his perch. "How's an old fellow supposed to sleep?"

"It's an emergency," said Cress. "Make a note of it."

"I know when I'm being mocked. Gotta love it. What's wrong?"

Just then Lolly Oakleaf poked her head out her window. "Cress Watercress! The noise! Finny is off roller-skating with his brothers. He said he was taking a break from you, anyway."

Cress shouted, "We need the doctor. Kip is worse."

"Dr. Oakleaf is making a house call to an ailing beaver at the dam," replied Lolly. "Dental distress. What can I do to help?"

"Come keep Mama company," said Cress. "She's in a tizzy."

Mrs. Oakleaf hurried down the tree with a few of the doctor's medicines in a paper sack. "I brought a thermometer, some throat lozenges, two bandages, and a mustard plaster," she said. "Also the sling for a broken arm. Just in case."

Kip was whimpering and looked yellowish. Mama told Cress to go outside and play.

As if this was a time for playing. Hop, hop, skip. Way fun? No way.

A few moments later, she was glad that Finny wasn't home this morning. Guess who came lopping along.

It was that rabbit, that devil-may-care rabbit. She was balancing the very same old picnic basket on her head. She saw Cress and headed toward her.

"What are you doing here with that?" asked Cress. "I'm going to get in so much trouble, you won't believe it."

"Nice to see you, too," said Nasty Nasturtium. She dropped the basket, and then she put a paw on her hip the way an old lady rabbit might, and pretended to moan with an ache. "I was doing you a favor. I thought you wanted it to carry ginger root for your stupid brother."

"He's not stupid," said Cress. "He's just a baby."

"Babies are very stupid," replied Nasty.

"Not Kip. Anyway, my mother said I had to take the basket back," said Cress. "The human beanpoles will be looking for it when they come for their doll-thing."

"They already came back. They tiptoed up to grab their stuff. The tablecloth, the doll, the wine bottle. But they left without the basket. I think they were too spooked by the Final Drainpipe to hang around and look for it. Anyway, it had rolled down the hill into the weeds. So here it is. A present."

Cress felt a little funny accepting it. "Did you see those humans?"

"Sure did. Briefly. They were still jittery about wildlife," said Nasty.

"Was that snake really there?" asked Cress. "Did you see him?"

"No. But I could sense him," replied Nasty. "That coiling tightness of a snake—you get a sort of a cousin feeling in your stomach. That's why I didn't come over when I saw you return with the basket."

Cress was appalled. "You were still there when I came back? And you saw me?"

"I thought you might come back and look for me," admitted Nasty. "I was hiding in the grass, waiting to be found. Hide-and-seek. But I was scared to come out."

Cress was sputtery. "Some old snake could have

eaten me, and you would have just . . . just sat there and watched?"

Nasty shrugged. "Gotta hand it to you. You were pretty sharp. First tucking yourself in the basket, then lobbing it at the fox, who was sniffing for baloney sandwiches."

Cress didn't know what to say. This was the worst friend she had not yet become real friends with. Maybe it wasn't worth it. Yet Nasty had brought the basket to her. And now, since the human beanpoles thought it was lost for good, they wouldn't be looking for it anymore. Cress could keep it.

Then Cress heard Finny and the others coming up the rising path, clanking their roller skates. "Can you hide for a moment?" she said. "My friend Finny is coming home, and, um, I think he doesn't like you."

"Nobody likes me," said Nasty. "That's the fun part. You should try it." But she climbed into the basket and pulled the lid down just before Finny, Brewster, Teddy, and Jo-Jo reached the crest of the hill.

"How's Kip?" mumbled Finny to Cress as his brothers scrambled up the tree.

"He's worse," said Cress.

"Oh," said Finny. It's hard to know what to say when someone is worse. "When he gets better, I'll teach him how to skate."

"He hardly knows how to walk yet," Cress reminded him. She didn't want to be rude to Finny. But she couldn't imagine Finny and Nasty getting along. Nasty was prickly, and Finny was—Finny. Cress said, "Maybe later on I can show you the new place to pick dead moths?"

"What a stimulating life I lead," said Finny. "Hunting for dead moths. But sure. Why not? So long." He scampered away, his skates bouncing against his bushy tail.

Nasty popped her head up. "That was awkward. Is he your boyfriend?"

"Of course not!" said Cress hotly. "And don't change the subject. I want to know why you didn't warn me about the snake. That's a lousy way to start being friends. Letting me hop into danger like that."

"Haven't had a lot of practice with friends," said Nasty. "Hence my nickname. But, look, I'm trying to make it cool. I brought you back your basket, didn't I? And on the way here, I picked up some news you might want to know about."

"News?" said Cress. She couldn't help but think about her father: she couldn't help it. Helpless, now and forever.

Nasty said, "I wasn't sure where the Broken Arms was because I never heard of you-all before. Anyway, as I'm looking, who do I run into but this big old sloppy-faced bear. Named Hunk or something."

"Tunk," said Cress.

"Hunk, Tunk. Whatever." Nasty rolled her eyes. "He called me the fairy princess of the forest glade or something. I said he had me mixed up with you."

"Why did you say that?" asked Cress.

"You're a lot more fairy princess than I am," said Nasty. "Anyway, he said he had a message for you."

Another message, another chance at hope. "What did you say?" asked Cress.

"I told him you lived at this dead old tree called the Broken Arms. He didn't know where it was, either, so I left him crashing about. Then the beavers down at the dam pointed this place out to me. That Tunk went lumbering about in the other direction, but he'll be showing up sometime, as soon as he gets his head on straight."

"Nasty," said Cress, "what is it with you? Sending a crazy old bear to someone's house? You have a whole lot to learn about how to be someone's friend."

"So you going to teach me, or what?" asked Nasty. "I got some time. But not too much."

Cress said, "Friends take time. First step, don't be mean to Finny or I'll bite your tail."

"This girl means business," said Nasty approvingly.

29

HIDE-AND-SEEK

So now Tunk was likely making his bumptious way to the Broken Arms. Did he have news of Papa? Or was he furious that Mama kept beating him to the honey bank and scarpering off with the freshest of supplies?

If the bear was angry, he might climb up the old dead tree. It would splinter under his weight. Mama and Kip would be crushed. Old Sophie Crabgrass wouldn't be able to scurry away, not with her bad hip. She and Manny would be flattened into mouse-shaped shadows of themselves. The squirrel family would be tossed like pine cones out into the field. Even Mr. Owl would tumble to his death. Only the songbirds, Romeo and Harriet, would escape.

"The bunny spirit of the forest has a headache, I see," said Nasty.

"Whatever you've done, I have to take care of it," said Cress. "Mr. Owl! Emergency call coming through. I need your help!"

"It's daytime," called Titus Pillowby Owl. "I'm having my daily rest."

"Well, wake up and smell the coffee," hollered Cress. "We're all in trouble. I'm calling for your advice."

The landlord ruffled his pinfeathers. "You don't have to shout. I may be blind, but I have perfect hearing."

"Tunk the Honeybear is on his way here," said Cress. "He might be angry about the honey Mama's been taking. He might attack the Broken Arms. We might all be in danger."

"That's a lot of mights," said Mr. Owl. "Someone's feeling mighty worried. Joke."

"No joke," said Cress. "What are we going to do?"

"You're known as the spirit of the woodland, apparently," said Mr. Owl. "You figure it out."

"But you're in charge!" cried Cress.

"Why do you suppose that?" asked Mr. Owl. "I'm only a landlord. True, I can scare off Monsieur Reynard, usually. And that old snake never dares slither up this way. My talons are sharp. But deal with a bear? I'm not qualified to take on a bear."

Cress thought Mr. Owl's voice sounded a little

uncertain. He stood on one foot and then the other, and then stepped back and forth again several times more. A nervous twitch. But there was no place he could walk to, no place he could fly to. He lived his life in a high and open prison, one without bars.

Nasty said, "Yo, Cress, that bear is a bit of a simpleton. He believes you're some kind of bunny fairy. Just tell him to go away or you'll put a hex on him." She looked over her shoulder. "Anyway, I'd like to stay and catch the fun, but I gotta run."

"Where do you have to run to?" asked Cress a little coolly.

"Someplace without bears," said Nasty. "I have my people to see, you know, here and there."

"Funny how you're always alone," said Cress. "Do you really have any people?"

Nasty stuck her head in the basket. "Nobody home in here," she said lightly.

"Stop kidding around. Where is your family?" asked Cress.

Nasty had a puzzled look on her face as if she didn't know how to answer the question. "I'll tell you a story if you tell me a story," said Nasty at last.

"My story," said Cress, "is that I am the real spirit of the woodland. There isn't any place called the Broken Arms, and I don't live there. And my father is still alive. That's a story, all right."

"Oooh, that's a good story," said Nasty. "I can't do one good as that."

"Try," said Cress.

"Mine," said Nasty, "is that my family moved and left me behind. I think there was a hunter, maybe, a human bean-pole. With a gun. My family scattered. I was playing hide-and-seek. When I came out from my spot, they were gone."

"Oh," said Cress in a small voice. She didn't know what a gun was, but it sounded risky.

So Cress and Nasty had both lost someone. But Nasty had lost everyone.

"I took a job as a maid for some skunky skunk," said Nasty. "That didn't work out. I quit. I've been on my own ever since."

"How can you stand it?" asked Cress. "Everyone being gone?"

As if Nasty wanted to avoid the question, she was suddenly gone, herself. She sped down the path, a blur of brown fur. Her paws drummed small thunder on the ground. She had a lot to learn about how to make friends.

Cress couldn't deal. She was getting no help from Mr. Owl. Cress couldn't bother her worried Mama. Fricassee Sunday, clucking to herself under the willow tree, would only be a blunder. There was nothing left to turn to but true friendship itself.

"Finny!" she called out harshly. "Olly-olly-oxen, all in free-ee. Where are you when I need you?"

"Where do you think?" replied Finny, bounding down the tree at once. "Right here."

30

TREE OF ALL SEASONS

Finny was all business. "I remember that old Tunk. We floated past him on our raft. He really did think you were a woodland sprite of some kind. He was a bit clueless."

"Clueless and dangerous," said Cress, "even if he doesn't mean to be."

"Well, he has a right to eat, too," said Finny. "I'm just saying."

Cress got in the basket.

"What are you doing in there?" asked Finny.

"Thinking. It helps." Somehow the tight space seemed perfect for right now. Safe.

"I'll stand guard, since I have nothing else to do," said Finny. "I'll watch for Tunk."

"I'll keep my ears open," called Mr. Owl. "Not that there's much need. Bears aren't stealthy. A deaf daffodil can hear them coming."

Cress thought about what Nasty had asked of her. The story, the story. Everybody's life was a story. Nasty's was a terrible story. Cress's was—was only partly terrible. Who knew what Tunk's story was?

There was a story in this basket, of baloney sandwiches and a child who had lost her doll, but her human beanpoles had come back to find it.

Stories everywhere. They grew thick as leaves on trees.

A story that Manny had shadowed for Kip, of wolves on the walls.

Fricassee made a possible story in an egg, over and over, every morning.

And Mama wove stories of moths and apples and roses in her tapestries of spring and summer and autumn.

Even the way Kip played with Rotty. "Bad Rotty!" Playing was a kind of story.

Everyone could make up a story except for Cress.

Make a note of it, make a note of it, she said to herself as if taking an exam. What do my notes say, all those notes I've made? For by now she had made dozens and dozens. So many, she could hang them all up on a spiderweb and they would become like fluttering leaves.

Then she had a notion. She poked her head out of the basket. "Finny," she said. "Tunk is looking for the dreary, barren Broken Arms."

"Can you be a little more polite?" he asked. "This place may be a dump, but it's home."

"We can disguise it," she said. "So he won't recognize it when he finds it." While Finny groomed his tail, Cress explained her idea. Dress-up for an apartment tree.

They dove into the basement flat. Mama and Mrs. Oakleaf were fussing over Kip. Mama was steeping a pot of ginger and honey tea. Lolly Oakleaf said, "This isn't the time to play indoors—get what you need and go back outside!" She was taking Kip's pulse with her little paw. She must have learned how to do that from her husband.

Cress and Finny grabbed as many bolts of Mama's recent work as they could hold. By the time they were done, they had fifteen new scarves and runners and tapering tapestries. They even grabbed the crumpled drapes from the old warren.

"If we're going to hang these up on the dead branches," asked Finny, "how can we lift them?"

Cress ran inside again and nabbed four or five skeins of wool. "I said OUT!" said Lolly Oakleaf. Mama looked like a bad drawing of herself that went outside of her own outlines. Frazzled.

Finny and Cress stretched out several lengths of wool in the grass. Finny cut them with his teeth. They braided and tied the lengths together to make a strong cord— almost a rope.

Then Cress fixed one end of the cord to the tasseled edge of the longest tapestry. Finny grabbed the other end of the cord in his mouth. He scurried up the trunk of the Broken Arms, the cord trailing behind him.

Nearly at the top, he darted out a bleached grey stretch of limb to where it leveled off. He looped the cord around the limb. Whistling "Here I go, look out below!" between his clenched teeth, he dove toward the ground. The cord trailed him still.

What a hero, thought Cress. My friend is a hero! I hope he doesn't become a very flat hero.

As Finny dropped with one end of the cord, the tapestry began to rise. Fold by fold, it unpleated itself off the ground. The cord was the pulley and Finny was the weight. The heavy cloth slowed down Finny's fall. When the weaving had reached its full height—twenty feet!—Finny was dangling at the ground. Cress caught him and grabbed the cord from his mouth.

Cress secured the cord underneath a rock. The narrow tapestry swayed. A story of leaves and moths nearly as high as the tree.

"Your mother does nice work," said Finny. "I'd have used a little more lemon yellow myself."

"Shut up," said Cress. "We don't have time to be critical."

Over and over Finny climbed and dove, and Cress caught him and made the cords secure, until the entire structure of the Broken Arms was draped with a fluttering fullness of color. That some scarves were orange and autumnal, some spring green, and some gold and blue as summer light only made the effect more magical.

This wasn't the Broken Arms. This was a tree of all seasons at once.

Cress stood under the pennants and looked at them. She heard Mr. Owl call out, "Ah, there you are. Over here, Tunk! Over here!"

She turned around. Tunk the Honeybear was hulking up the slope toward the Broken Arms, which in all its sham and glamour was dressed for a miracle.

31

SPARKLIO!

Tunk was dressed for an audience, too. He wore his epaulets and his necklace of bee corpses. He also sported a headdress of deer antlers. He was a bear on a mission.

He walked with his regular heavy tread, but his face was uplifted. He carried an old glass soda bottle in one paw. Cress could just make out the name on the side. In worn red letters it said SPARKLIO!

"I'm looking for the Broken Arms," said Tunk to Finny and Cress. "But this can't be it."

"No," said Cress in as brave a voice as she could manage. "The Broken Arms is, um, down on its luck. But as you can see, *this* place is a total holiday."

"Joke!" called Mr. Owl. "Tunk, you're reached the right address. Welcome to the Broken Arms."

Finny and Cress dropped open their mouths at the betrayal by their landlord. What was he thinking?

Just at this moment, Mrs. Oakleaf came barreling out of the downstairs flat. She didn't see Tunk at first. "Red alert!" she called. "Jo-Jo, run to the beaver dam and see if your father is still there. Teddy, try the heron pond, where there was that outbreak of fish rash. Brewster, scamper upstairs and tell the songbirds we need an all-points lookout for Dr. Oakleaf. Emergency! Now! Move, people, move!"

The squirrel brothers sprang into action. Mrs. Oakleaf turned to give sharp instruction to Finny and Cress, but her eyes fell on Tunk, looming there like a brown mound of menace. And Mrs. Oakleaf fell prey to that sudden paralysis of squirrels. The mere instinct that befalls them when grave danger comes too close to do anything else.

She froze. She had no choice. If she'd seen Tunk coming, she would have been prepared. But the alarm about Kip Watercress had disturbed her natural caution.

"Hurry!" called Mama from indoors, unaware of the breaking news happening only a few feet away.

Tunk wasn't put off by anxiety and commotion. He

didn't even notice. He squinted at all its colored trappings and said, "I know this is the right place. This has to be the Broken Arms."

"Bingo," called Mr. Owl.

"How come you think that? How come?" asked Finny, trying to drown out Mr. Owl.

"Lookit," said Tunk. "Who else but the noble spirit of the woodland could live here, in this very tall fairy palace? All these flags, all these colors at once. It's magic."

Cress wanted to get inside to Kip and Mama, but she couldn't put everyone else at risk. Then and there she changed her mind and gambled on honesty. "Look, Tunk," she said. "Mr. Owl is right. This is the Broken Arms. I'm the one you're looking for. You mistook me for some secret sprite of the forest once, and I let you believe it. But it isn't true. I'm just a girl rabbit. Cressida Watercress. And I have to go home, so, like, could you go away now? Please? I'm asking nicely."

It was the first time she had called the Broken Arms home.

"You think you're just a regular bunny," said Tunk, peering at her. "But how do you know you're *not* the spirit of the woodland? I think you are. You're in disguise to yourself. You'll figure it out. I don't care. I don't even care if you believe me. I believe in you, O Cress Watercress, special magic secret agent of Hunter's Wood. How else could you live in a place that looks like this?" He gestured to the bannered apartment tree.

"Oh, that, that's just us having fun," said Cress. "Costuming."

"Never underestimate the power of good design," added Finny.

"I brought you a tribute," said Tunk. "My offering of honor to the spirit of hereabouts."

He held out the glass bottle marked SPARKLIO! Cress could now see that there was something inside, some sort of golden substance.

"Your mother and I have been tussling over the honey supply," said Tunk. "Usually she gets there first and is gone before I show up. I'm a late riser. Sometimes so late that it's early the next day. But I came to tell you something. I have it from the queen bee that the hive is about to split. This happens sometimes. A delegation is going to emigrate and set up shop elsewhere. This will double the honey supply. Neither of us needs to go hungry."

"Great, thanks, goodbye," said Cress.

"No," said Tunk. "You're not listening. Take my gift."

He held it out. She reached out her paws for SPARKLIO!

"This is the hive's unique, reserve, limited-edition honey," said Tunk the Honeybear. "They only make it for special occasions. They made some last night as the hive is getting ready to divide. The queen bee allowed me to take it as an offering to the woodland spirit of the forest. It has special properties."

"Great," said Cress. "I'll make a note of it. Bye."

"Medicinal stuff," said Tunk. "Are you listening? Don't you have a little brother who suffers a complaint of one kind or another? Croupiness, wheezing, something?"

Tunk had paid more attention than Cress had given him credit for. "Well, yes," she admitted. "But I didn't think you'd know about that."

"I follow the gossip," he replied, plumping up his epaulets. "I may not be a crown prince of anything, but I'm not just a bump on a log. I hear what the birds are tweeting about."

"Tunk," said Cress. "I owe you an apology for being scared of you for too long."

"I like it when people are a little scared of me," said Tunk. "But it's more useful for you to be scared of Monsieur Reynard and his cousins. Or of the Final Drainpipe. Sure, I can be a bit brusque and excitable, and I sit on small animals by accident. Still, except for the occasional fish supper, I'm a vegetarian."

"But why would you even bother to help us?" asked Cress.

"Aren't you the one who lost her papa recently?" replied Tunk. "I couldn't stand by and watch you risk losing your baby brother, too."

Cress couldn't speak. She held the SPARKLIO! to her heart.

"I'll see you out," said Finny.

"I'm already out," said Tunk. He looked up into the ceremony of flags and pennants above. "All the seasons at one time. If that isn't magic, what is?"

He walked away.

Only now Cress noticed that in addition to his antlers, his dead bees, and so on, Tunk was wearing a sash woven of fresh ivy. Maybe he was the spirit of the woodland. Maybe they all were.

Later that day, Cress had an answer to Tunk's question—what is magic? The magic was recovery. The queen bee's gift of the special, reserve, limited-edition honey, when mixed with the fresh ginger root dug up from under the gingko trees, packed a punch. It cleared up Kip's lungs. His fever dropped. His sleep became regular.

Mama dragged herself outside to draw a fresh breath of air. She looked up at her work.

"Not bad, is it?" she had to admit. "Sometimes I seem to know what I'm doing."

Dr. Oakleaf was just coming up the path, exhausted from his long hours on the job. Too many emergency shifts in a row. He was surrounded by three of his sons. Brewster carried his valise, and Jo-Jo carried his tail. Dr. Oakleaf said to his wife, "Hey, honey, snap out of it," and Mrs. Oakleaf blinked and was herself again. "What's up with this?" asked the doctor, gesturing above him.

"Redecorating, I guess," said his wife.

"I liked it better the way it was," said Dr. Oakleaf, and went inside to put on his slippers and have a wee drink.

32

BEING FOUND

By the next day, things had settled down. Kip felt so much better that he learned to brush his own tooth. (He only had one so far.)

The squirrel family helped to undecorate the tree. Mama still had a living to make at the fall market. She didn't want her hard work to get spattered with evidence of the songbirds' comings and goings.

The big fat spider on the enormous web didn't seem to mind when Cress or her mother came to pick off dead moths. Both Mama and Cress preferred harvesting moths who had already died to luring live ones to their death in hot candle wax.

They were up there one morning, the three of them. Kip wanted to throw Rotty into the web to see if Rotty would stick. The old spider was glaring at Kip as if daring him to try. Mama said, "Cress, I need you to tell Kip a story. Or take him for a walk. We can't afford for him to wreck the web."

"I don't do stories," said Cress. "We'll go on a ramble."

"Not far," said Mama. "Stay within earshot."

Cress grabbed Rotty and said, "Tag!" Kip toddled after her, bellowing. First they played Toss the Rotty and then Bury the Rotty in the Mud, and then they played Wash the Rotty in the Brook.

Then they started to play hide-and-seek. Since Kip could only count to three, when it came Cress's turn to hide, she had to do it fast.

When Kip closed his eyes to count, peeking only a little, Cress ran to get behind a nearby rock the shape and color of a turtle shell. She wondered if it really was a turtle and, if so, whether it would mind her being there. But the space behind it was already taken up. Nasty Nasturtium was crouching there, down low.

"ONE," yelled Kip.

"Are you spying on us?" whispered Cress.

"No," said Nasty. "Yes. I don't know. I'm just playing hide-and-seek, too."

"Hiding from what?" asked Cress.

"Everything."

"And seeking what?"

"You know what."

Cress did know what. She said, "Look, Nasty. I don't think I can be your sister. We just don't have the room. Besides, your family might come back looking for you."

"Sure they might," said Nasty. "Any day now."

"TWO," bellowed Kip.

"But we can be real friends," Cress said. "If we work harder at it."

"Oh," said Nasty, "you're going to start making the rules?"

Cress replied, "The rules are already made up. Pretty basic. Friends take care of each other. They don't run away. They don't make fun of each other. That's about it. It's not a tricky concept."

"So I have to be, like, all nicey-nice with that squirrel-boy, too?"

"Finny's my friend, too," said Cress. "No apologies. Get used to it."

"TREE!" called Kip. "Weady aw not, Kippy COME!"

When Kip found both Cress and Nasty hiding in the same place, he laughed and laughed.

The rock yawned. It turned out to be a real turtle. It took them for rides. Nasty told Cress that she was currently

living in an abandoned warren in a riverbank on the other side of the hill.

"Oh," said Cress. She didn't ask any more about that. She didn't want to know if it had three rooms and a pantry and a back door and its own carrot garden.

Cress told Nasty about the visit of Tunk, and the Tree of All Seasons, and about Mr. Owl giving the secret away. "But why?" asked Nasty.

"From way up there, Mr. Owl can hear just about everything," said Cress. "It turns out he knew that Tunk had the special high-quality honey. He heard the bees buzzing about it. He was trying to help Kip get better by signaling our location to the bear."

"I thought you said he was mean," said Nasty.

"Everyone's got secrets," replied Cress. Then she told Nasty the secret of Mr. Owl's broken arms. Well, wings.

Nasty said, "So he can see everything and hear everything but can't ever join in. I know just how he feels."

"How does he feel?" asked Cress.

"Like—" said Nasty. Then she tried again: "Like. I don't know. Lonely. Like the whole world is a story. And he's not a part of it."

"He's a part of the story. You're a part of the story," said Cress. Just then Kip fell off the turtle, and Mama started to call them for supper. "You want to come home and eat with us?" asked Cress.

"No. I want to get back before dark," said Nasty.

Cress felt bursting with happiness. She needed to do something nice for someone, even if Nasty wouldn't accept an invitation. "You know what?" she said. "We should find a way to help Mr. Owl be included more. It's fun to play hide-and-seek. But it's more fun to be found."

"You're the woodland spirit of the forest," said Nasty. "Got any ideas?"

"Maybe I can figure something out," said Cress. She was fresh from the success of inventing the magic tree. "I'll let you know. See you around." A terrific and normal thing to be able to say to Nasty.

33

A Mysterious Creature

Mama," said Cress as they hopped down the hill from the big web. "I think Nasty is hiding out in our old warren. What if we went back to live there? It could be our home again. I'd have company when you went out at night. And Nasty would have a rescue family while she waits for her own family to come find her."

Mama pursed her brow. "I don't know if we can trust Nasty any more than we can trust Rotty. That poor child has a lot to recover from, and a lot to learn. It's not her fault, but I'm not up to the task."

"You're mean," said Cress with a certain amazement. "I didn't know that. I'm shocked at you."

"Cress, you're a sweetie to care so much about Nasty. But even good folks can't do every good thing they can imagine doing. They just can't. We can't take Nasty in, and I can't go back there. You understand what I'm talking about. I just can't."

"It used to be home," said Cress in a whining voice, but she knew when she was licked.

"The Broken Arms is home now," said Mama. "For the time being. Until that old dead tree blows over in a high wind. Or until we get behind on our rent again and get kicked out. The Broken Arms has to do. And it's not so bad, is it? I've come to like our neighbors. Even Lolly Oakleaf. She's good in a crisis, I'll give her that much."

When they were back at the apartment tree, they met Manny. He was sitting outside, whittling a yo-yo. "You've got company," he said. "I let her into your place with the spare key. Hope you don't mind. A mysterious blonde. She wanted to be out of the spotlight of sunshine. Said you'd been expecting her."

"Manny," called Sophie from the fire escape. It was the first time Cress had ever heard Sophie speak. She had a lovely foreign accent. Maybe Manny was the only word she could say to her husband. Maybe it was enough.

"Gotcha, cupcake," he replied, and shuffled along, taking his yo-yo for a walk around the world.

"You're out of your wits, Manny," said Mama, hurrying forward.

"Hey, Mrs. Watercress," called Mr. Owl. "You have a stunning blond visitor."

"We were warned," said Mama in an aside to Cress. "The downside of apartment living. Everyone knows your business."

Cress was cross. She yelled, "Mr. Owl, always listening in on everyone. Your secret is out, too, did you know that? You're not blind. I know that. Because no one can hear that someone is blond."

"Oh, you'd be surprised," said Mr. Owl, but in a smaller voice than usual. Cress had startled him and hurt his feelings.

So now she felt bad. It was never-ending, this carnival of feelings. So tiring. Mr. Owl was all alone in his penthouse. He could never play hide-and-seek. Never had once in his life. It wasn't his fault his wings were useless.

Right then Cress got her idea for Mr. Owl. Just as her mother opened the door.

The daylight fell upon the too-large carpet that still rolled up in curls on either side of the room. Upon one of them, as if it were a doctor's waiting room, sat a dazzling figure in golden tresses. Wearing a chinchilla.

"I've said it before and I'll say it again," said Mama. "You have some nerve."

"You have to help me," said Lady Agatha Cabbage. "I was trying to put in some platinum highlights, and I got carried away."

"I got carried away, too," said the golden chinchilla. "Like it or not."

"You have no right to be here," said Mama. "You kidnapped my only daughter."

"A little misunderstanding, tut-tut and so what, all is forgiven, and I move on without holding a grudge," said Lady Cabbage. "Can you help me? You're a designer of sorts."

"No," said Mama. "I don't do makeovers. I prefer the natural look."

"I mean," said the skunk, "may I buy one of your shawls? To cloak myself in? Tone down my glory? The drabber the better."

Mama said, "I may not be flashy, but I don't do drab, either."

"I'm putting it poorly," said Lady Cabbage. "The problem is I shine like a beacon and don't look like a skunk anymore. I look like—like something else."

"A mess?" suggested Mama.

"A clump of dried-out golden moss?" suggested Cress.

"LOUD!" shouted Kip.

"A target," interrupted the chinchilla, sounding over-wrought. "We've become targets. Any number of bald eagles have been hanging around Two Chimneys trying to get a glimpse of the new tender morsel in the forest. They don't realize it's just Lady Agatha Cabbage."

"Beauty is a curse," said the skunk. "So I need to bring it down a bit."

"Tough," said Mama. But Lady Cabbage had begun to examine the goods. She found the drapes from the old house. Periwinkle ferns against a background of pale oak leaves.

"This is perfect. Perfectly ordinary. How much?" asked Lady Cabbage.

Mama looked the skunk up and down. "I have my price," she said slowly. "No bargaining. Take it or leave it."

"Shop people," said Lady Cabbage, sighing. "What's a skunk to do? All right, put me out of my misery. Name your price already before I have a heart attack."

Mama said, "Your chinchilla."

"My what?" Lady Cabbage was incensed. "I'd be lost without my chinchilla."

"Darling, you're so lost already," said her fur. "I say it's a deal. I'm tired of hanging around with you. And hanging around you."

"It's so hard to keep good help," said the skunk. She rotated the chinchilla till its little front and back paws showed. They were clasped together with a silver chain.

Mama gasped.

"Don't be all huffy. It's a charm bracelet," said the skunk, and unlocked the little creature's legs. "It's worked like a charm all this time."

"I can't believe it," said Mama. "You locked up your fur collar, too?"

"For security. Now listen to me," said Lady Cabbage. "You are a wonderful weaver. You do fabulous work." The shawl did indeed look both elegant and a little homespun against her golden fur. "Don't question my practices. I am a cut above."

"I don't like you," said Mama. "And I don't think I ever will."

"You be you," said Lady Cabbage, "and let me be a skunk." She sallied out, leaving the chinchilla behind. "I'm still looking for a parlor maid, don't forget. Though if your daughter gets much older, she'll have to apply as a lady's companion."

The chinchilla stood in the middle of the carpet looking shy. "Do you have a name?" asked Mama.

"Willa," said the chinchilla.

"I should have guessed," said Mama.

"Mama," said Cress, going up and leaning against her side. "You can't give Nasty a home here, but you free a *chinchilla?*"

"Willa is going to be our parlor maid," said Mama. Before anyone could become outraged, she said, "JOKE."

Willa the chinchilla played tug-of-war with Kip and Rotty. As Cress pressed the dead moths on waxed paper for delivering to Manny, who would take them to Mr. Owl, she told Mama about the idea she had had. A big surprise for the landlord. To thank him for leading Tunk to the Broken Arms. To give Mr. Owl a chance to join in.

"It's risky," said Mama. "Some people don't like surprises. You could end up hurting his pride."

Cress was pretty sure she could carry this off. Anyway, she wanted to try. She got out all her little papers and made notes all night long.

34

A Note of Surprise

Two days later everything was ready. Everyone could come. No one had other plans. It would be the must-attend event of the season.

"I do hope you know what you're doing, sweetie," said Mama.

"What's the worst that could happen?" said Cress. "Now that we know Mr. Owl isn't going to swoop down and carry me away."

"He could still turf us out," said Mama. "We'd have to find someplace else to live."

"Turf us out? For giving him a surprise party? If he's that crazy, we'd be better off living someplace else."

"It's not that easy, Cress." But her mother was trying to be open-minded and not so tense all the time. "I understand about hide-and-seek. You explained it well. Everyone deserves to be found. Even a grumpy landlord. So I've got your back. Good luck."

Fricassee Sunday had gone ahead with Dr. and Mrs. Oakleaf. They were seeing to the refreshments. The other tenants of the Broken Arms hung around as if it were an ordinary day. All watching out of the corners of their eyes.

Finny and Cress tied their strong cord around the handle of the picnic basket. Cress took a deep breath and signaled to Romeo and Harriet.

The songbirds picked up the other end of the rope in their beaks. Together they carried it to the topmost branch of the Broken Arms, just a step below Mr. Owl's perch. They crested the branch and flew down the other side. Finny and his brothers waited to receive it.

"Okay," said Finny. "Let's do this." Cress gave him a paw bump.

She hopped into the picnic basket and held on tight. Finny, Brewster, Teddy, and Jo-Jo began to haul away at the other end of the cord. In scary jerking movements, the basket rose into the air.

No one could pretend it wasn't happening. Even Mr. Owl, who was often asleep at this time of day, turned to face the branch around which the wool cord was straining.

Up in the air Cress went. Past the Crabgrass flat, where Sophie waved through the window. She gave Cress a a wink and an encouraging grin.

Past the Oakleaf place. Cress could see in the open door of the front porch. The apartment was a tip, with acorn shells, playing cards, and popcorn spilled all over the place.

Even past the bird nest. Cress was glad she wasn't a bird. Or a squirrel. She never wanted to be this high again. Being off the ground was not a delicious miracle. It was awful.

Cress couldn't look down until she realized that maybe from up here she could see her old home. In a way, if she could see that, her whole life would be visible from one glance.

But the world had other ideas. It had leafed out. Up high was like being in clouds of green paper shapes. This was like a water world, with its own system of shadows and currents. She felt she was floating in several ways.

Then, before she could become grossly ill, she came level with Mr. Owl's horny talons. "My, my," said Mr. Owl. He stared at her with no pretense of being blind. He seemed hunted, and offended. "To what do I owe the pleasure of your intrusion?"

"I've come to invite you to a party," said Cress.

"What a hoot," said Mr. Owl. "Or do I mean a hootenanny? Joke. Thanks just the same, but I don't get out much."

"I know," said Cress. "I've arranged to give you a lift."

With trembling paws, she reached out and grabbed his branch. She hugged the central spoke of the tree. "You get in. The Oakleaf boys will lower you to the ground."

In an entirely different tone of voice, Mr. Owl said, "My dear child. You are insane. What made you think of this?"

"Let's not talk now," said Cress. She had to close her eyes. This high up, the wind was fierce. "Just get in and get going, so they can send the basket back for me."

Mr. Owl had his pride, as Mama had predicted. But pride can also mean knowing how to accept a brave gift. Maybe one you don't even want. Without further comment, the landlord stepped forward into the bottom of the picnic basket.

"Going down," said Mr. Owl. His eyes were wide and wet. And down he went.

It took forever for them to raise the basket again, but eventually they did. Cress got back in. Down the basket dropped, jerkily, until it bumped against the ground and fell over on its side. Cress was politely sick on the grass. Everyone looked in the other direction. She wiped her mouth on some fresh clover. Finny took the lead and said, "Forward!"

The songbirds led the way through the woods. Behind the squirrels and the rabbits, Mr. Owl walked with full strength and confidence. He carried Kip piggyback.

The super and his wife fell behind almost at once because of Manny's cane and Sophie's hip.

The party for Mr. Owl was set up beside the spiderweb near the gingko trees. There would be food, and games, and prizes, and hide-and-seek. Willa the chinchilla was there, and Fricassee Sunday, and Tunk the Honeybear, who didn't seem quite to know what was going on.

Lady Agatha Cabbage showed up in her new shawl. She went up to Nasty, who was looking very hip in the doll sunglasses. The skunk said, "You look familiar. Don't I know you from somewhere?"

"Lady," replied Nasty, "you don't know me. And you never will."

"Well, I'll trade you my charm bracelet for your glasses," said the skunk.

"Deal," replied Nasty. "I could use some charm."

Lady Cabbage put on the plastic sunglasses. They made a great improvement: there was less of her to look at. Behind her dark glasses, Lady Cabbage swanned around like an actress at a premiere.

But before the food, the fun and games, Cress made a little speech.

"Mr. Owl," she said. "We want to thank you for being patient with us when we are late with our rent. You live above us and know everything, but being up there isn't like being down here. We wanted to give you a chance to join in."

Mr. Owl cleared his throat. He was very moved. "You're all terrible, so I'm raising your rent" was the only thing he could say. He didn't even have to say JOKE. Everyone knew.

Then Cress said, "You always say to make a note of it. So I did. Everyone else can make things up, and I thought I should try, too. I made you a song."

At this, everyone turned to the spiderweb.

All of Cress's small pieces of paper had musical notes drawn on them, one per page. Hundreds of them. They were hanging on the sticky web. The big old spider beamed from the corner as if she had composed the music herself.

"You've written me a song?" Mr. Owl was nearly stricken with shock. He tried to flap his wings, but they were still broken. They always would be. "Cress, you have to sing it for me."

"Mr. Owl," said Cress, "I wrote it. But I can't sing it."

"Why not?" asked the landlord of the Broken Arms.

"Because," said Cress, "I don't read music."

So the songbirds sang the song. Apparently it was a duet. Cress thought it was pretty good. Nasty thought it was lame, and said so. Finny bit Nasty on the tail, and then they all played tag while the grown-ups sat down and were lazy and talked about life. As if there was anything left to say about it.

35

HEREABOUTS

Before she left the neighborhood, Fricassee Sunday came by the Broken Arms to say goodbye to the Watercress family. Mama was out taking Kip for a stroll. Cress was the only one home. She was fiddling with some paper and a pencil. "I'm moving in with Lady Cabbage," reported the hen.

"You're nuts," said Cress. "She'll make you her maid."

"I admire her verve?" said Fricassee. "So I am going to be a lady's companion. Equal status. She'll let me borrow the sunglasses sometimes. And she's going to buy some of your mother's hangings? To dress up the place. I insisted. What are you doing?"

"Scribbling," said Cress.

"That's what I thought? It looks like hen-scratchings. I mean that in a nice way? Are you writing another song?"

"It might be," said Cress cagily.

"Well, you should write a story," said the hen. "Make it about me?"

"I don't know how to make a story," said Cress.

"It's like making an egg, I think?" said the hen. "Just sit there until it comes out."

"But I wouldn't know what to put in a story," said Cress.

"Blunder and wonder," suggested the hen. "That about covers it. Anyway, I shall miss you all, but we'll stay in touch. I'll be okay with that skunk. I'm smarter than I look?"

"I bet you are," said Cress, and bent back to her task.

So, she thought, as the hen left, this is how things are in Hereabouts.

That's what Cress had started calling the new neighborhood, now that she had seen it once—just once—from the air. From a bird's-eye point of view, Hereabouts made sense.

Right in the middle of Hereabouts, the Broken Arms poked up, dead but full of life, on a bluff of boulder. Nearby was the grassy meadow, the fair woods, the willow, the stream. In another direction lay the mossy glade and the honey tree.

On the other side of the stream, a little farther off, rose the hillside with its gingko trees and its big old spiderweb and its rock outcroppings.

Farther off was the pond. Below that, Two Chimneys.

All of this, Cress understood, was really Hunter's Wood. Beyond it, on all sides, lurked the edges of the risky human world, filled as it was with hunters and hideous dolls.

The old warren, though—the place they had come from, where they had lived as a family of four—that wasn't in Hereabouts. It never could be. It remained in the past. Nobody ever talked about going back there again.

The rest was just neighbors in their simple lives. Day by day and sun to moon. Each day hatching a little different from its sister. The story of life scrabbled on, good and bad together.

When Nasty promised not to chain Willa up with the charm bracelet, the chinchilla went to stay with the orphan rabbit. At least for a while. Neither of them liked to be alone at night. Little by little the chinchilla developed sandy-colored roots, and her golden hairdo began to fade.

Willa taught Nasty a few manners. Nasty taught Willa how to curse.

Finny and Cress stayed the best of friends, and that was that, no more to be said, and it's none of your business, anyway.

Cress often met Nasty in the woods or on the hillside. They had agreed not to mention Nasty's family or Cress's father. It worked better that way. The two rabbits played hide-and-seek, or just hung out and talked. Nasty liked to mock others. A little guiltily, Cress laughed. Nasty was good at being Nasty. Cress was still learning to be Cress.

Oh, Cress and Nasty, Nasty and Cress. It wasn't an easy friendship, and it never would be. When Nasty showed up at the Broken Arms, Finny kept his distance. But at least Finny and Nasty rarely bit each other's tails anymore.

Once, after Nasty had flounced home in a burst of temper, leaving Cress cross and Kip in tears, Mama said to Cress, "That child has a lot of—"

"Nerve?" supplied Cress.

"Spunk," said Mama after a pause.

"I thought you were going to say 'nerve,'" said Cress. "You don't like her, Mama, do you?"

"I said 'spunk.' She has a lot of spunk," insisted Mama.

Cress pressed on. "You don't like her."

Mama paused. "I like spunk."

"That's because," said Cress slyly, "you have a lot of spunk, too."

"You better believe it," said Mama. "Tell that to the Final Drainpipe."

Who had still not shown up, and maybe never would. Or not until the end. Whenever that would be.

But meanwhile, the days kept blooming in all the soft-colored weathers of Mama's loom.

The moon rose, over and over, a surprise each night it was visible.

Sometimes it was tiny, the eyelash of a hummingbird. Sometimes as fat and soap-bubbly as a badger washer-woman. Sometimes it hid behind the clouds. Sometimes it disappeared entirely from the clear sky.

Cress never entirely got used to the changes. But she began to get it: that changes in the moon, like the constant changes in her heart, were normal. And would never end.

The regular sadness that, out of kindness, Cress had stopped talking about to Mama? That would never change. Cress was learning to live with it.

Cress was babysitting Kip one evening while Mama was away visiting some of her thousand cousins. They were home alone, because Cress was older now. Also, Kip had outgrown his asthma and he could talk, more or less. Cress said, "Kip? Do you remember Papa?"

Kip shrugged.

"I want to know," said Cress. "Do you remember him, Kippy?"

Kip said, "I remember Papa when you tell me stories about him."

"When I tell you stories," said Cress, "I remember him, too."

So Cress told Kip the stories she could recall, the ones about when they were still a family together, with Papa, Mama, Cressie, and baby Kip. How Papa disappeared. How the rest of the Watercress family moved to the Broken Arms. And everything that had happened since then. They shut the door for good, and they never went back. But they never forgot.

"We never will forget," said Kip staunchly, eating a real carrot, not Rotty. Mama had taken up stitchery, and now she used the old bedraggled stuffed carrot as a pincushion. "No, we won't forget," said Kip. "Make a note of it."

Cress did. Once her song had been sung by Harriet and Romeo, Cress had pulled all her musical notes off the spiderweb. On the back of those pages, she scribbled anything she could remember. She'd decided she could make up something all by herself. Fricassee Sunday was right. It just came out. She wrote down the story of how she and Mama and Kip had come to be in Hereabouts.

When it was done, she realized she had actually said very little about who Papa was to them. But what was there to say? Only this:

Papa was nice. He liked carrots. He was average size for a rabbit. His looks were ordinary and his habits mild. He was more than good enough. He loved his family.

So this is the story she wrote. She has tried to leave out the boring parts. She hopes you like it. It is almost all true.

She has called it after her own self, which she knows is a bit stuck-up.

But it's the only title she could think of right now. It's her first try.

Cress Watercress.
By Papa's daughter,
Cress Watercress.

THE END
(but not the Final Drainpipe)